Sweet Clarinet

I would gladly have welcomed death with a passion—as long as it stopped the pain. 'Oh, God, let me die, please, please, let me die. I'll say my prayers every night, honest, if only you let me die.'

Billy thought growing up in wartime was fun: the fiery skies, exploding factories, the noise of the blitz, playing among the rubble of the bombed houses. But then a bomb fell directly on the shelter where Billy and his mother had gone to escape the bombardment and changed Billy's life for ever.

Billy wakes up in hospital, horribly burned and longing for death—angry at a world in which he will always be a freak, an object of horror or pity, an outcast—until a precious gift from a soldier who is also disfigured gives him hope and a reason for living.

JAMES RIORDAN was born in Portsmouth and grew up there during the war. After he left school he worked as a postman, a barman, a crate stacker, a railway clerk, and a double bass player before doing his National Service in the RAF, where he learnt Russian. After demobilization he did a joint honours degree in Social Science and Russian at Birmingham University. He gained a teaching certificate from the London Institute of Education and then went to Moscow for five years, studying and working as a translator. Back in England he lectured at Portsmouth Polytechnic and Birmingham and Bradford universities and from 1989 at Surrey University where he is now Professor of Russian Studies. He h̶a̶s̶ ̶w̶r̶i̶t̶t̶e̶n̶ ̶. . . ̶a̶c̶a̶d̶e̶mic books on Russian social is̶. . .̶s̶ of folk-tales, and a number ̶. . .̶ based on his own wartime ̶. . .̶ children.

Sweet Clarinet

OTHER OXFORD FICTION

Sweet Clarinet

James Riordan

OXFORD
UNIVERSITY PRESS

OXFORD

Great Clarendon Street, Oxford OX2 6DP

Oxford University Press is a department of the University of Oxford.
It furthers the University's objective of excellence in research, scholarship,
and education by publishing worldwide in

Oxford New York
Athens Auckland Bangkok Bogotá Buenos Aires Cape Town
Chennai Dar es Salaam Delhi Florence Hong Kong Istanbul Karachi
Kolkata Kuala Lumpur Madrid Melbourne Mexico City Mumbai Nairobi
Paris São Paulo Shanghai Singapore Taipei Tokyo Toronto Warsaw

and associated companies in Berlin Ibadan

Oxford is a registered trade mark of Oxford University Press
in the UK and in certain other countries

Text copyright © James Riordan 1998

The moral rights of the author have been asserted

First published 1998
Reprinted 1999
First published in this edition 1999

British Library Cataloguing in Publication Data available

Cover photography: R. A. Simpson Photographic Studios

ISBN 0 19 275050 X

3 5 7 9 10 8 6 4

Typeset by AFS Image Setters Ltd, Glasgow
Printed in Great Britain by Cox & Wyman Ltd, Reading, Berkshire

To my dear daughter Catherine

Contents

1
The Bomb

The bomb came through the roof of the air raid shelter. An ugly big grey cigar, snub nose at one end, fan tail at the other. It sliced through the centre of the flat brick roof and dropped on the floor with a CLANG.

We watched fascinated.

The image could not have lasted for more than a split second. Yet in that time I saw stars twinkling in the night sky, smelt brick dust, and heard the drone of aeroplanes. Funny how all the senses can work overtime together.

Then came an explosion of the most wonderful bright colours: orange and green, scarlet and yellow, violet and indigo, all mixed together as on an artist's palette. Warm air, like a midsummer breeze, swept through the chilly shelter; yet nothing stirred. No noise. No movement. Not a whimper. Everything was as still as the grave, the calm before the storm.

Like a black and white snapshot, the flash lit up chalky-white clown faces: of little children in white flannel nightdresses, old men and women in long black coats and scarves, elderly couples draped in sepia brown blankets. Grotesque masks with dark gashes for eyes and mouths. A lad of about my age stood opposite as still as a marble statue, his mouth gaping, his eyes staring.

Then, all hell broke loose. And HELL it was!

The blast rammed my ear-drums through my head, flattened my nose against my skull, rattled every bone in my body. I was hurled against the wall and had all the air sucked out of my lungs. A red-hot wind swept over me, turning a cold night into a scorching Saharan afternoon.

Yet I felt no pain. Not a twinge.

The bomb had landed slap bang in the middle of a crowd of fifty or sixty people summoned from their beds by the air raid siren. Dead on target—not that a huddle of kids, women, and old men was much of a target.

Instinct had made me cover my eyes with my hands. Now intense pain forced me to take my hands away and hold them on my lap palms down. Then a strange thing happened. I watched in horror as the skin on the backs of my hands bubbled and browned like cheese on toast; slowly the skin melted away to charred ends of finger bone.

This couldn't be me. It must be Guy Fawkes on a bonfire. But there were no flames here, just agonizing, piercing, searing heat.

HELP ME!

Desperately I looked round for my mother. But from my corner I couldn't recognize a soul. What I saw will remain with me forever, a horrific nightmare stamped on my mind's eye. People were burning. They were trying to rip off their clothes, beating at their heads, arms, legs, backs to kill the flames.

Human fireballs dancing a crazy jig before crumpling to the floor. Children screaming for their mothers. Men whimpering like puppies. Women caterwauling at their own helplessness.

As if to draw a merciful curtain over the scene, a black, choking cloud spread from the centre of the shelter, swiftly blotting out the dance of death. No longer could I see white eyes in black swollen heads, charred arms held out in prayer.

At last my numb mind awoke. I knew I had to get out. And fast. Yet as I tried to pull myself off the floor, grasping the bench beside the wall, I found my hands oddly slippery, like bars of soap. On the ends of my arms were blubbery balls of raw meat.

Using my knees and feet to lever myself up, I stood facing the wall of black smoke, wondering which way was out. Just then I felt a faint ripple of air on the bridge of my nose—that must be the escape route to safety, life, moonlight, fresh air.

Shutting my ears to the screams about me, I stumbled forward, choking on the smoke, bumping into twisting, groaning human forms; it was almost impossible to find a way through. Yet instinct, call it what you like—a cold-blooded will to survive—drove me on, treading on a moving staircase of writhing bodies hidden by the black pall.

Hands clawed me back, thrust me aside in a frenzy to escape.

By now I was fighting for air, calling on every breath left in my lungs, battling for short gasps. My nose and mouth pressed into my sleeve so as to avoid taking down the hot black smoke. I struggled to keep moving, inch by inch, two steps forward, one step back.

All at once I was there, standing before the door. I felt the cool, blissful night air on my face. With one last charge, I knocked someone aside, lurched through the opening, and fell into the roadway.

I gulped air into my lungs in great big dollops.

Never had fresh air tasted so sweet.

Then a black cloud descended and I sank into a tub of burnt treacle.

2
Growing Up in Wartime

Growing up in wartime was fun.

For us kids even the falling bombs were an exciting game; and since our city was a naval port, it got a good pounding from Jerry, lots of incendiaries, fiery skies, exploding factories, bombed houses.

I liked the noises of the blitz best: the Nee-YAWWLL-oooll of the siren, the POOKKH-POOOKKKHHH of exploding bombs, the dull drone—dummm-dummm-dummm—of planes, and then the YEEE-awwll, YEEE-awwll of the All Clear. And so to bed.

After the raids Charlie Foreman and I used to explore musty-smelling houses, climbing rickety stairs and poking around in the rubble for bits of bodies. We never found any, though once a fat grey rat jumped out of a chimney and scared the living daylights out of us. We thought it was Old Nick come to grab us!

One Sunday dinner time a bomb fell on the church across the road. It was a 'dump bomb', one left over from blitzing the dockyard; the pilot dumped it down anywhere for fear of a clip round the ear when he got home to Jerryland. It knocked out all our windows, including the fanlight over the dinner table.

We were all sitting round: Grandad as always in his brown check cap, Grandma in her apron, Aunty Doris and Aunty Rose, Mum; Aunty Edie had just hurried in from St Mary's where she was a nurse. The fanlight glass showered down on our meat, cabbage, marrow, and roast potatoes; but we still ate them!

It being dinner time saved the old vicar of the bombed church. He was sheltering under a stout oak

4

table when the bomb fell and the roof caved in. Not a scratch, lucky beggar.

I don't think he had any dinner though.

The gas masks we had to wear during air raids made us look like creatures from outer space. We had to put them on when the siren wailed and we made a dash for the sandbag-covered Anderson shelter in the back garden—usually in the dead of night. We needed to put on our wellies as the shelter was knee-deep in rainwater. And it stank to high heaven.

After a while, we abandoned our tin shelter and used the communal brick shelter down the street. And that's where fate changed the course of my life—but that came later.

When a raid was on, white searchlights criss-crossed the black sky and puffs of grey or orange smoke from pom-pom guns smudged the moonlight. In the daytime barrage balloons floated in the sky like giant sausages with elephant ears.

The nearest we came to war was our stone fights on bombed sites; sometimes we built bonfires on the rubble, burning Hitlers instead of Guy Fawkeses, and we held contests to see who had the best Hitler. Then we'd strut around the fires with one finger under our nose, right arm in the air, shouting, '*Sick Hail! Sick Hail!*'

Food was rationed in the war, so we had to queue each day for meat, shoving, bellyaching, afraid supplies would run out. The coupons in our ration book only allowed us one bag of sweets a week; but we could get a penn'o'th of chips and fish scraps at Bert's Fish & Chip Shop, wrapped up in a greasy newspaper. Shake the big tin salt-cellar and vinegar bottle over them and they'd smell and taste delicious. All washed down with ginger beer.

You could buy some things for a farthing or ha'penny—like an Oxo cube which we'd suck on our way home from school, or a purple aniseed gobstopper which we'd pass from mouth to mouth. You could get toffee apples for a farthing each or a ha'penny worth of loose barley sugar, or 'cough-no-more' lozenges at tuppence a bag. Other favourites were jelly babies and toffee which came in big slabs that had to be broken with a little hammer. I especially liked liquorice sticks because they made your mouth go black and Mum thought all my teeth had come out.

There wasn't a lot to eat, so we war kids used to go down to the soup kitchen. Since it was right opposite St Mary's Hospital, we reckoned the stew was made of dead men's legs. I know for a fact that the dripping on the bread came from melted down dead bodies.

My grandad was a chimney sweep: each tea time he'd trundle his old bike through the house, with long black spiky brushes tied to it. I can still smell and taste the gritty soot. No matter how hard he scrubbed his face, the soot would still ink in the wrinkles up to the brim of his greasy brown cap. He never took it off, even indoors; I reckon he wore it in bed too!

There were eight of us living in the two-bedroomed house, so we had to sleep two to a single and four to a double bed, two up, two down, in one room, with Gran and Grandad in the other. It was snug and warm, but you always had someone's cheesy toes in your face. On Friday nights we used to take turns having a bath in a long zinc tub in the scullery—using each other's soapy water topped up with a kettleful of boiling water from the hob.

When you wanted to 'spend a penny', you had to go outside to the backyard lavatory, night or day, rain or shine. It was the only place you could be alone, reading the scraps of newspaper we used as toilet paper.

Our grandad even died in the lav. That was in the middle of the war: Aunty Rose couldn't find him one morning, so she went into the back garden, lifted the latch on the lavatory door—and poor old Grandad tumbled out. He'd been there all night. It was a nasty shock for Aunty Rose!

His was the first dead body I ever saw; when he was laid out in the front room, beside the big aspidistra plant, I peeped in to see if I could see his soul going up to Heaven. This spooky experience served me well: for whenever I had a fit of giggles at school, I only had to think of that dead body and my face went straight at once.

The street was my playground. We'd chalk the pavement to play hopscotch, or we'd jump over sticks or play marbles in the gutter—often losing a prized bull's-eye down the drain. Lamp-posts were our rounders' base—until the gaslighter chased us off or we broke a window. On the way to school I'd dribble a tennis ball in and out of dog muck; and in the school playground we'd play football or five stones. In autumn we'd thread conkers on shoe laces, take turns to hit each other's and see whose conker lasted longest.

After school, me and my mates would meet to play tag or gingerbread—knocking on someone's door and running away. We never played games with girls—they had their own groups, playing ball games, piggy-in-the-middle, or skipping.

Since I lived by the sea, I used to be a mudlark in summer; I'd roll up my trousers when the tide was out and scrabble for pennies in the stinking mud down by the Hard. Poooh. It didn't half pong! Still, it earned a few grimy coppers for a stick of barley sugar or some mint humbugs.

On our street there was an old man with a racking cough and wheezy chest—said he got gassed in the Great War. I'll never forget him telling us one day that whenever he saw us mudlarks it reminded him of his mates struggling in the mud of the war trenches. 'God bless you, sonny,' he used to say. 'I hope to goodness you never end up dying in the morass of war.'

He died before the war was over—he wasn't to know that millions upon millions of young men and women all over the world died in the mud . . . the sea . . . the skies . . . the gas-chambers.

Searching the Rubble

The morning after the bomb was sunny and warm. A crowd of ashen-faced onlookers stared, dazed, into the still smoking rubble. It was as if they expected an arm or head to thrust its way through the broken bricks, and a dusty body to rise from the dead. Some of the crowd were neighbours, some relatives; all knew the victims—a roll call of the dead and missing had already been made.

They all lived cheek by jowl in two cosy red-brick terraces; it was their community shelter that had gone up in smoke.

A mobile canteen was dishing out mugs of tea to the silent crowd, while wardens in tin helmets sifted through the debris scattered half-way down the road. God knows what they hoped to find.

There certainly were miserable possessions that needed rescuing; someone might claim the battered teddy bear with one leg, a brown carpet slipper, a dusty purse containing tuppence and a silver threepenny bit, a scorched cloth cap, a dusty yellow scarf.

Mercifully, the medics and the Home Guard had toiled all through the night under arc lamps to sift out human remains. Not that much was left or recognizable. How could so many bodies vanish into thin air? There was not enough human debris to fill more than six or seven stretchers. The rest had disappeared off the face of the earth. God give them rest.

Right after the explosion a mere ten out of the fifty or so night refugees had survived: ten who had somehow crawled and scrambled to safety from the blazing inferno, or who had been pulled out still breathing. But six had lasted only a few hours; they mostly suffocated from smoke-clogged lungs.

'They're the lucky ones, Jack,' remarked a grim-faced orderly to his mate as they poked around in the rubble. 'At least they snuffed it nice and quick.'

'Yeah, you're right, Ron,' muttered Jack through a damp hanky covering his mouth and nose. 'Poor bleeders, didn't know what hit them, they must have gone peaceful like.'

The two men were numb and tired; they'd been up all night, ferrying buckets of water and sand along the human chain from the Static Water Station, the SWS, to the blazing shelter. They had finally smothered the last flames as dawn broke: ironically, one red fire went out as another flared in the morning sky.

And they had done their stint tending the injured and dying—that was the most harrowing task of all. There was one consolation for their night's work—they had pulled a baby live from the rubble: miraculously it was unharmed, cradled in its dead mother's arms.

In the early hours of the morning, they had also come upon an elderly couple in the only part of the shelter still standing; the pair hadn't a scratch on them, though both trembled violently from shock. Jack and Ron had forced some hot sweet tea down their parched throats and that had revived them.

'God help that young lad,' continued Jack, raking over the night's horror in the ashes of his mind. 'He was terribly burned. What sort of life will he have even if he survives?'

Ron was silent. He just shook his head sadly.

3
Pleasant Dreams

When I woke up I was lying in bed with just a sheet on me. My legs were covered in bandages, my hands in rubber bags. I could feel some sort of gauze over my face, with slits for eyes, nose, and mouth—or, at least, where they ought to be. Only dimly was I able to make out light and shade. Perhaps I'd gone blind?

Although I was swimming in and out of consciousness, in my waking moments I could feel waves of excruciating pain wash over my entire body. I had no idea how badly hurt I was, even whether I would live. Or was I already dead? At that stage I had no desire or energy to find out.

I remember once seeing a film about war, *All Quiet on the Western Front*, where this German soldier had lost his legs; he was lying in hospital unaware of his injuries, but feeling the worst pain in his feet. The funny thing was he had no feet! I hoped those were my legs and feet underneath the bandages . . . They didn't half ache.

Sleeping merged with waking, so that I never knew what was real or what a dream. Perhaps the air raid had been a horrible nightmare and I'd wake up, bounce out of bed and hug Mum tight: she'd wonder what was up. Trouble was, the feel and smell of the bed were different from home. And this stank of hospital with its pungent antiseptic smells.

In my brief visits to the real world my body never let my mind dwell on the whys and wherefores. So intense was the pain that it overwhelmed everything, drove all thoughts out of my head. My one urge was to escape from the torture—by any means possible.

I would gladly have welcomed death with a passion—as long as it stopped the pain. 'Oh, God, let me die, please, please, let me die. I'll say my prayers every night, honest, if only you let me die.'

The only outlet for agony was my mouth. I screamed and screamed and screamed. Well, I tried: I opened my mouth and throat, got the bellows working on my lungs, made all the motions of a scream. Whether anything came out I'll never know.

I heard nothing. I saw nothing. No one came in answer to my cry for help. Or so it seemed. Now and again, true, I glimpsed shadows flickering in slow motion, like dim lantern slides, round my bed. They might have been angels come to take my body up to Heaven—or were they there just for my soul? I never could work that one out.

The only other craving, besides release from pain, was for a drink. I'd have sold my soul for a gulp of cold water. I now know what it is like to be lost in the desert, crawling on hands and knees, the sun beating down, your lips all scabby, your tongue dry, your throat parched. Water! Water!

In my sleep, if such it was, I fought my way through a mass of bodies time and time again, now surging forward, now falling backwards. I trod on a nest of writhing serpents whose coils wound round and round my ankles, holding me back; they slid up my legs, over my belly, up and up, coiling round my neck, squeezing all the breath out of me.

My fevered mind brought back tastes and smells of smoke which swirled about me like thick fog, forcing hot grit and cinders into my nose and mouth, so that I could no longer breathe fresh, cool air. Then I was drowning in warm black treacle which forced its way past my lips and through the gaps in my clenched teeth; it tasted bitter sweet, rolling over, under and round my tongue, cloying, oily, thick, down my throat in solid dollops, down, down into my lungs. It filled them to the brim and overflowed into my boots.

Those were some of the pleasanter images. At other times, my mind served up stark pictures of faces screaming, bodies burning, hands melting. I could smell burning flesh and singed hair. Again and again and again. The boy statue opposite me in the shelter was a constant companion to my nightmare. At times he was smiling bravely at me, giving me courage; he seemed so utterly calm and detached.

At other moments he was shrouded in a bright rainbow arc that went right round his body, rather like the boy Jesus in the Bible pictures I got from Sunday School. Only I couldn't see his face, just a jagged black hole of a mouth, like a dark cavern in a cliff.

Those were some of the vivid images of nightmareland, images that no child should rightly see, they should have had an H certificate. But war is no respecter of age or sensibility. Thankfully, nightmareland sometimes led into dreamland, the Land of Oz, warmed by sunshine and coloured by happy memories.

I dreamed it was Christmas. Father Christmas had come down the chimney in the middle of the night—he didn't seem to worry about air raids—and filled an old sock with an apple, some walnuts, a packet of sweet cigarettes, and chocolate money.

All the family came round for the Christmas party; we had it in our living room decked out with paper chains glued together with flour-and-water paste. We played blindman's buff, pin-the-tail-on-the-donkey, and ducky-ducky; then we had a sing-song with Aunty Doris on the piano.

In another dream I snuggled down in a plush seat at the Majestic Moving Picture House—known to us as the Fleapit or Bughutch; we called it that because we all felt a bit itchy when we came out. The picture houses round our way all had fancy names—Majestic, Regal, Odeon, Apollo, and they smelt deliciously of candyfloss. Sometimes an organ would rise up through the floor like a genie, and play in the interval between the black and white films.

It was only later I realized you had to pay to get into the cinema. We used to hang about the side door and, when someone came out, we'd 'bunk in'. It's a wonder our little caper didn't bankrupt the film industry.

Several of my dreams featured winter evenings at Aunty Rose's after she'd moved into her own house. We used to roast spuds on the coal fire and toast bread on long forks: what a lovely smoky-yeasty smell! Aunty Rose and I would gaze into the flames and see all sorts of fantastic sights: beautiful fairies, long-bearded gnomes, caves full of rubies and pearls, ugly ogres and horned devils. Then Aunty Rose would tell our fortunes in the tea-leaves of an empty cup: I always ended up marrying a pretty blonde.

As a special treat, Aunty Rose would make me a 'doorstep' sandwich with quince or plum jam. There only seemed to be quince and plum jam in the war—I put some down for Tiddles the cat once and we didn't see him again for a week.

Aunty Rose had a framed letter from the king above her bed, saying how sorry he was that her husband, Sidney, had died in the war—a U-boat had sunk his ship off the Isle of Wight; all six hundred men had drowned. He was only twenty-three.

The trouble with my dreams was I got pitched abruptly from half-complete memories into noiseless screaming pain; then after a while I sank back into nightmares—and off I went again on the agonizing merry-go-round. Oh, God, please let me die!

4
Goodbye to Mother

How long my in-and-out of waking, in-and-out of nightmare lasted I don't know. Nor do I know how close I sailed to the whirlpool of death. I really didn't care. All I can say for certain is that one day I came back.

The pain still hurt like hell, my body was swaddled like an Egyptian mummy, and I felt terribly drowsy: I just wanted to sleep and never have to wake up. But I could see! I dimly made out a blurred bedpost, a fuzzy fly on the wall, a zigzag crack in the ceiling; and slowly but surely the images came into focus.

So at least I had my eyes.

And my ears—since I could hear cars revving outside the window, someone whistling out of tune, seagulls whooping and mewing, a bluebottle bouncing off the window pane in increasing rage: plop-bzzzz-ping-bzzzz-bonk!

I wasn't deaf. But was I dumb? That was the next item on my agenda.

I tried a one-note noise: 'aaahhhh . . . ohhhh . . . eeehhh.'

It sounded low and hoarse, like a donkey gargling; the effort strained my tonsils and lungs. Yet there was no mistaking the croaky sound.

My oohhs and aahhs must have carried to other ears, for in no time at all a nurse came scurrying in. When she saw me blinking my swollen eyelids and dribbling down my bandaged chin, she gave me a great big toothy grin.

'Oh, so you're back in the land of the living, Billy boy,' she said. 'About time too, lazing about in bed all day long.'

As if my Rip Van Winkle slumbers weren't enough, I yawned and . . . went straight back to sleep. Only later did I fully appreciate what the nursing staff had to endure—what with scabby bodies like mine and the nauseating stench of putrid flesh; having to bathe me each day and soak off the bandages—though there was nowhere to catch hold of me because of the burns. They never complained, never displayed any disgust; and most were young girls, wartime volunteers, with no proper training or preparation for the horrors of war.

Real cheery cherubs they were.

When I next came to, my first thought was of food. I was ravenous. I managed to utter the one word 'f-f-f-ooo . . . ' I couldn't quite reach the final 'd'. But the nurse got the message and swept out in a starchy bustle and smell of disinfectant.

She was soon back, triumphantly carrying a tray with a bowl of egg custard—a rare treat in wartime. I'd have preferred fish and chips, though they wouldn't have preferred me.

She spooned half the custard into my mouth. The rest got spluttered all over the sheet and down my bib.

'Good lad,' she said, as if to a baby learning to eat.

Then, realizing I was a growing man—all of eleven years old—she added, 'That'll put hairs on your chest.'

I promptly went off to sleep, dreaming of sprouting a bushy black beard and matted chest overnight. When I awoke, matron in her stiff navy blue uniform stood unsmiling at the foot of my bed. She was looking down at me like a haughty high priestess in her temple; and when she spoke, her words were as hard as nails. That was her manner—I expect she was one of those high-class horsy ladies doing her bit for the war effort, a modern Florence Nightingale.

She meant well, even if she was unused to the wounded hoi polloi.

'There's someone to see you, Riley,' she said curtly. 'Are you up to receiving visitors?'

I did my best to nod. Making noises was still too exhausting. One mouthful at a time. But my mind was working overtime, making up for the delayed actions.

Who was it? Mum? I hoped against hope that she was alive; but the nagging realist in my head said otherwise. Dad? But he was at the North African front: he'd gone over on the first troopship. Surely they wouldn't send him back just for me?

Perhaps the king had decided to pay me a visit to save stamps on a letter: 'Well, hello, William Riley, isn't it? Keep your p-p-pecker up, laddie. That's the sp-spirit.'

Matron went out and soon returned with two figures in coat and skirt: one outfit was black and musty, the other was rosy pink and smelt of new-mown grass. As they swam into view, I saw it was Gran and my sister Iris.

Gran was from the Irish side of the family, as stubbornly independent as Paddy McGinty's goat. When the siren wailed, she had refused to toddle down the road to the air raid shelter.

'Whist, I'll put on me wellies and stand in our garden shelter,' she'd said. 'If that bomb's got my name on her, she'll find me wherever I am, so she will.'

A born fatalist, our gran. But it had saved her life.

Mum had packed off fifteen-year-old Iris with other evacuees in early forty-three; I was due to follow a few months later but what with first measles, then mumps, I got held up. Iris'd only gone some ten miles down the coast, to sleepy old Nutbourne; but Jerry wasn't interested in flattening cowsheds and turnip fields out that way.

Iris and I had always had a love-hate relationship; we'd fought like cat and dog for as long as I could remember. I thought she was a bitch; she called me a scallywag. I was glad to see the back of her and was dreading evacuation within a hundred miles of my sister.

My two visitors were plainly ill at ease.

As matron returned, I heard Gran ask under her breath, 'Is that him?'

It was more the tone of her voice than the question that irked me, as if I was a stiff laid out in the morgue. Who the hell did she think it was? The Michelin Tyre Man? Of course, it's him! It's me, ME, Em-Ee, your grandson, Our Willie, as you used to call me. I can see, I can hear, I can even talk, so watch what you say!

But I didn't have the strength to say boo to a goose; anyway, she wouldn't understand.

Iris just stood there gawking, wrinkling her nose as at some nasty smell, one arm on the bedpost, a look of repugnance on her freckled face.

'What's it like under all that wrapping?' she asked at last.

'Well,' said matron stiffly, punching my pillow while searching for an apt reply, 'IT'S still your brother.'

IT'S!!! I'm a *he*, not the cat's father. HE, HE, HE—a living, breathing, feeling human being!

With a sigh, my sister said grimly, 'I suppose he can't be any uglier than he was . . . '

How wrong she was.

It was matron who reminded them that the figure in the white gauze suit could see and hear everything. He wasn't a sack of rotten potatoes, even if he smelt of them.

'William can hear you,' she said. 'And he can converse a little, though he tires easily. So don't overstay your welcome.'

With that she swept out to fetch a vase for the flowers they had brought.

Gran and Sis sat down uncertainly on the wooden chairs by the wall. Neither made an effort to move them closer to the bed. I could sense I was an awful shock to them, confronted by this pass-the-parcel object who didn't smell too nice. All that linked me to them was the name-tag 'William Riley' clipped to the iron bedhead.

An awkward silence followed.

'E-o, Gra . . . ' I managed to squawk at last.

I don't know what she was expecting, but the noise almost knocked her off her seat. She stared, went to say something, then burst into tears. Shaky words flowed through the tears.

'Willie. Oh, Willie, my poor Willie. God save you, musha, live, oh live.'

'Come on, Gran,' said Iris, putting her arm round the frail shoulders. 'This isn't helping him, is it?'

My next grunt made things even worse.

'Mum . . . '

It rang out loud and clear, like a rifle shot. There could be no mistake. Iris and Gran looked at each other helplessly, then stared down at the floor. Luckily for them, matron came in with the vase of bluebells, and Gran appealed to her for help.

'Er, he's asking about his ma,' she said, her eyes full of pain.

'Then tell him,' said matron bluntly. 'William's a big boy.'

Matron's departure exposed the two women again, and they lapsed into silence.

'Is'e det?' came the disembodied voice.

The sound might be jumbled, but the meaning was clear enough. Painfully so. It was Iris who finally screwed up the courage to reply.

'Mum died in the air raid, she didn't suffer.'

I wept inwardly.

'Oh, Mum, no, no . . . '

After a few moments' silence, Gran found her voice. The painful secret was out, and she could speak more easily.

'You're lucky to be alive, Willie.'

A voice in my head responded at once.

'No, I'm not, I'm lucky I'm not dead.'

There was a big difference. But the words never saw light of day. Though angry at the world, and even at Gran and Sis, I was alive, and presumably I had a life to live.

'I ti'e . . . ' I muttered.

In case that sounded ungrateful, I wanted to add, 'Thanks for coming; please come again.' It came out as, 'Ta-a-a . . . '

They understood. As both got up, thankfully, neither spoke, neither gave me a farewell wave. Gran, however, went to pat my shoulder, thought better of it, and touched the pillow instead. The last image I have of her is of kindly grey eyes blurred with dewy tears, full of pity and pain. All she had left to share her grief with was her Catholic God; and he hadn't been much use to her so far in her hour of need.

Iris marched straight out, staring stonily ahead, not giving me a backward glance. She'd done her duty, and she wouldn't need to come back for a few months. Her thoughts about me must have been frantically confused. Better to push me out of her mind than try to sort them out.

My eyes were smarting so much, I closed them gingerly and sailed off in my private paper boat down a dark tunnel, bobbing along on a troubled sea of drowning figures. In my sleep I was fighting off grasping arms and steering past mouths that opened and closed like goldfish gullets. Desperately I pushed the bodies back down into the water and shut my ears to their gurgling screams.

Then all at once I woke up, fully conscious. To my surprise I saw the shadow of a woman at the foot of my bed; she was looking down at me, smiling that warm, brown-eyed smile that had calmed me ever since I was a baby.

'Hello, Mum. Thanks for coming. I haven't half missed you.'

She smiled, but said nothing.

There was so much more I wanted to say; yet just as I went to speak again the figure slowly faded away like a momentary shaft of sunbeams. All I managed to mumble was, 'Bye, Mum.'

When I finally came out of my feverish dream, I felt quite safe, as if a great load had been lifted from my mind. Never again did I feel that I wanted to die; nor did I even believe I would.

I had said goodbye to my mother and she had taken away the guilt I felt for surviving while she had died.

5
The Old-New Face

It had to come. The day when the bandages came off to reveal what was left of me, my old-new face. Even now the first sight of my new self is too painful to describe.

Of course, I'd gone through all the preliminaries, imagining how I might look. But nothing prepared me for the truth. This was it. This was me. Gruesome Gus.

I just wanted to hide, to shrink into my flaps of skin and disappear for good; I dreamed of living alone on a desert island for the rest of my natural—not that there was anything natural left. I thanked my lucky stars that Mum wasn't there to see me; and the news that Dad was 'missing, presumed killed' only swelled my relief.

And if ever I doubted the full horror of what my own eyes saw in the mirror (I had to beg the doctor to let me face the truth), I only had to see the shock reflected in the eyes of matron and the nurses—like finding a dog turd in your bed. Poor souls, it wasn't their fault. It's human nature to shrink from unpleasant sights. How would I feel looking at a horror mask?

The surgeon did his best to reassure me.

'Look, William, it's best now to air the skin and tissue. That should heal the scars quicker. You'll look a sorry sight for a while. Be brave and bear with it. As soon as we get some new flesh on you we'll press on to the next stage, make you as handsome as Gary Cooper.'

'How do you turn Frankenstein's monster into Gary Cooper?' I wondered grimly.

Anyway, I wanted to be me, not some American cowboy.

Gran came to see me almost every day. Not once did I catch a flicker of fear on her wrinkled face. She always looked me straight in the eye, even when I was moody and depressed, impossible for company—which was just about all the time.

My sister too, on her rare visits, showed more patience than I imagined she possessed. Perhaps she was seeing someone else, not the awful little brat she'd grown up with.

All the same, there was nothing they could do or say to cheer me up or rescue me from self-pity and self-disgust. I had sunk too low into the well of gloom, and no one could reach down far enough. Even Gran's sad news of my dad failed to weigh heavy on me—everyone else was way down the list of priorities. First, second, and third were ME, ME, ME. The rest of the world could go to hell for all I cared. I was overwhelmed with anger, at how unfair life was, at how I had no future in the normal world.

I was a freak. F - R - E - A - K.

It must have been a relief for Gran and Sis when I was finally moved to a special convalescent home deep in the country—hidden away behind tree and bramble so that no one would have to set eyes on its inmates. Just imagine going for a quiet walk in the woods and stumbling upon Sleeping Beauty's castle. Yet instead of sleeping beauties, you found yourself walking among zombies with no ears or chins or noses, monsters whose human features had been shot or burned away, walking freaks eaten up by some foul pest called war.

It was at this ill-named Boniface Home that surgeons began the slow process of rebuilding my face. I had to make regular visits to the burns unit of the nearby hospital; the plastic surgeon assigned to me was a specialist in treating burns victims, and he'd seen it all. So I was just another hank of flesh and bone to Mr Whiteway: to cut, chisel, graft, mould; to turn twisted, gnarled, charred wood into a smooth fine sculpture.

23

He had no sympathy for my down-in-the-dumps
mood.

'Listen, son, I can improve your looks,' he told me on
the first visit, 'but you'll never be an oil painting. It'll
take time and I'll need your help. I'm a healer of sick
bodies, not a mender of men's souls. So the sooner you
banish the blues, the quicker you'll aid both of us.'

His matter-of-fact tone only strengthened my
hostility. As the weeks and months passed, I was able
to hobble from my solitary cell down the long corridors,
through the ornate halls and elegant drawing rooms of
this once fancy country estate. I bumped into—or,
rather, did my best to avoid—fellow pariahs. And I soon
got used to the exhibits in our chamber of horrors.

It was weird. So accustomed was I becoming to the
abnormal that I almost came to see the normal as
grotesque, as different from the rest of humanity. But
there were plenty of reminders of the standards society
set for Beauty and the Beast.

Even the war's end had little impact on our home.
One day matron assembled us all under the chandeliers
and announced in a graveyard voice, 'I have some
important news. You will be pleased to know the war is
over. Three cheers for our gallant soldiers! Hip-hip-
hooray! Hip-hip-hooray! Hip-hip-hooray!'

We didn't exactly raise the roof. No one even thought
to ask who'd won. All the same, there was a keen sense
of relief that blanketed us all. No more bombs, no more
killings, no more sad entries to our home . . .

A few days later we were treated to a special party: it
was a sunny May day when we were led out on to the
normally sacred front lawn. We were to take our places
at long trestle tables set end to end and covered in white
tablecloths. Matron and the nurses then brought out cakes,
trifles, jellies, and endless plates of bread and marge,
while a few grown-up visitors danced about in paper
hats and funny masks. Flags and bunting straddled two

leafy oaks above the tables—by the look of the flags they hadn't seen light of day since the relief of Mafeking!

It was as good an excuse as anything for a beano.

Though the war had come and gone, peacetime made no difference to my life. The guns and sirens may have fallen silent, but my personal battlefield was here; the fighting for life continued; the casualties of war tiptoed shamefacedly through our elegant home.

Peacetime, however, did mean lots of books and comics, even if they were all second hand, donated by distant do-gooders—*Wizard*, *Hotspur*, *Dandy*. Apart from that there were schoolbooks. School came to us and we kids formed classes in the fine chandeliered ballroom. Unlike normal school, we had fairly small classes of ten or a dozen pupils; all tossed in together. The youngest was eight and the oldest sixteen.

It didn't seem to matter, especially as the older ones worked with the youngsters. And since we had little else to do, we spent much of the time reading, and doing jigsaw puzzles, building Meccano cars, poring over homework. No doubt we turned out to be brainier than most kids of our age since we rarely went out to play. Not that we would become judges or doctors or professors, someone in the public eye. Come to think of it, we could hardly become sales staff at Woolworths either.

The trouble with all the comics and books was that in them only the baddies had cruel faces and twisted smiles like ours, while the goodies hadn't a blemish on their prissy mugs. Same with the films we watched every Saturday afternoon; and the Bible classes at Sunday school. And the framed pictures in our country house . . .

Everywhere we looked it was Beauty and the Beast, handsome cowboys and scarfaced Indians, clean-cut Yankees and evil Jerries or Japs, smart cops and mean-looking desperadoes.

The clash of images depressed me. I withdrew deeper and deeper into my own world, refusing to eat or attend classes for days on end. Finally, I stopped speaking: when anyone asked me a question I refused to answer; when anyone greeted me I just scowled.

I was building a wall around myself, brick by brick. Inside my fortress I felt safe, I could rant and rage, simmer and hate.

No one ever visited my room since I had pinned a notice to the door: PRIVATE. KEEP OUT! Most kids soon learned to avoid me; they had long since stopped inviting me to join their games of table tennis or tiddly-winks, let alone birthday parties.

Yet one day I had a visitor. My room was at the end of a long dingy passage, and next door to me was another room which at one time had been the dressing room to my master bedroom. It was occupied by a girl six months older than me: and I hated her. She was one of those goody-goodies, forever acting the Good Samaritan to other kids. What was worse, most seemed to go along with her, bringing their problems to her room.

They would tune in to the wireless and turn up the volume for *Appointment with Fear*—'This is your storyteller, the man in black . . . ' Real spine-chilling stuff, which I secretly loved.

When they played Ludo and Snakes and Ladders, though, they kicked up such a fuss it drove me round the bend. I'd bang my fist on the wall, but it didn't do any good. You'd think that with a face like hers she'd do the decent thing and keep out of sight. Yet looks didn't seem to bother her—perhaps she never gazed into the mirror. I overheard a nurse once tell the cleaner she was the only one of her family pulled alive from their burning house; it took a direct hit from an incendiary bomb.

Anyway, late one afternoon she barged right in and

plonked herself down on the end of my bed. I pretended she wasn't there.

'I've brought you a fairy cake,' she said with a cheery grin. 'I made it myself, with pink icing and a cherry on top.'

She was obviously as pleased as Punch.

I glowered.

After an awkward silence, she continued in a kindly voice, 'Billy, I know how you feel. Let's be friends as well as neighbours.'

I held my tongue. How *could* she know how I felt? What a cheek! She wasn't going to buy me off with a measly cake.

After a while, when it became clear I wasn't going to give in to her charms, she got up and went out, leaving the fairy cake in its paper cup on my bedside table.

From then on she came in just about every day, almost always with a little present, a bribe to get me to talk. It didn't work. But she never stayed more than a minute. She wouldn't say much. How could she when she was just talking to herself? I continued to cower behind my wall of silence—though I did eat the cakes and sweets she brought!

One day she brought a book.

It was new and wrapped up in a brown paper dust-jacket. The book was a collection of true stories about heroism in war—so she said, babbling on about its contents.

Now, if I had a weak spot, this was it. I spent all my spare time reading: Biggles' stories, *Treasure Island*, *Tom Brown's Schooldays*, *Ivanhoe*, *King Solomon's Mines*, and, of course, all the comic adventures of Desperate Dan, Billy Bunter, Wilson the wonder runner who had discovered the elixir of life. (Fat lot of good that would have done me!) I suppose I enjoyed escaping into the fantasy of other people's lives, anything to avoid facing up to mine.

She was crafty, my neighbour. She knew my
weakness. And she had cunningly left a cigarette card
in the book, marking one particular story. Curiosity
made me read the first few lines. I was hooked at once—
like choosing a kitten from a litter, something you can't
resist.

If the printed word can alter someone's life, then that
story had such an effect on mine.

A Soldier's Tale

You hear a lot of stories about heroism in war. Most go unrecorded. Those who've been through it rarely boast or even talk of their experiences. They've seen things that are best forgotten. All the same, war strips a man bare, peels off the outer cover, like dead skin after sunburn, leaving just the inner core, the real self. And when a man's at war, constantly facing death, he rises above his everyday self. Naturally, the core is tougher in some than in others; yet even cowards rise above themselves—no one wants to let his mates down.

This story is about a young soldier, a lance-corporal—a quiet, ordinary lad from a mining community. In Civvy Street he was an unassuming fellow, tall and broad-shouldered with an honest face; but the army seemed to turn him into a veritable god of war.

Standing in his tank, head and shoulders above the turret, he was a Lancelot or Arthur, a fair knight riding into battle. He was one of those people whose very presence could inspire: you only had to see him vault to the ground, pull off his helmet to free his thick fair hair, damp with sweat, wipe his smoke-streaked face with a rag, then smile broadly from the sheer joy of living. And you smiled broadly too: it was great to be alive!

Terry Clough was proud of his mining background.

'The thing about coal miners is dignity and self-respect,' he used to say. 'It's in your skin like coal dust.'

We knew Terry was engaged to a girl from the same village, though he said precious little about her and never joined in the general banter about girls; but he did once say his Mary had promised to wait for him even if he returned on one leg.

Nor did he talk about his part in the war.

'I don't like even thinking of such things,' he'd say with a frown.

But I heard plenty from a member of his tank crew, Driver Jim Wigglesworth; he had more than a few tales to tell about his mate Terry—he didn't earn bravery medals for nothing. But it was Jim's story of his bravest battle of all that I want to tell you about.

One time, soon after D-Day, when the Jerries were on the run, Terry and Jim's tank was hit by a shell: it killed two of the crew outright. A second shell set the tank on fire. Driver Wigglesworth managed to escape after the first shell, but Terry wasn't so lucky. It was then that Jim climbed into the burning turret and managed to pull out Lance-Corporal Clough—he was unconscious and his clothes were a mass of flames. Jim had only just dragged him clear when an explosion ripped the tank apart, hurling the turret a full fifty yards down the road.

Desperately Jim threw handfuls of loose earth on his mate's head and clothing to smother the flames, then he carried him on his back from one shell-hole to another until he found a first-aid post.

'Why did I do it?' he said afterwards. 'Because he's my mate.'

Well, Terry Clough survived and didn't lose his sight, though his face and hands were so badly burned that bones poked through in places. He was laid up in hospital a good nine months: one operation followed another. Plastic surgery eventually rebuilt a nose, lips, eyelids, and ears. At the end of the nine months, after the bandages were removed, he looked in a mirror at a face that was his—yet no longer his.

The nurse who had handed him the little pocket mirror turned away and wept. As he put down the mirror, he muttered, 'I've seen worse.'

But he never asked for the mirror again. Instead he

would often feel his face with the tips of his fingers, as though trying to trace the new contours.

When the medical board declared him unfit for active service, he went straight to his Commanding Officer and requested permission to return to the front.

'But you're disabled,' said the CO.

'No, sir, I'm not,' he replied. 'I'm disfigured, and that doesn't stop me fighting.'

Terry noticed that the officer, a battle-hardened veteran who'd fought in the Great War, hardly looked at him during the interview—that brought a grim smile to his blue slit of a mouth.

He was granted a month's leave to complete convalescence at home before returning to his unit.

It was early April when he finally arrived by train at the station. He had expected to catch a bus, but decided to walk the ten miles to his village. The ground was covered with light snow; it was cold and deserted everywhere. The biting wind kept tearing open the flaps of his army greatcoat and howling about his ears. By the time he reached the village it was growing dark.

He passed the coal mine and at once caught the familiar smell of coal dust in the air; past the Working Men's Club, the pub, and the chippy, turn the corner—sixth house in was his parents' home. With a happy smile of anticipation, he quickened his step; then suddenly he faltered, slowed down, and stopped dead in his tracks. What on earth was he doing? Thrusting his scarred hands deep into his pockets, he shook his head grimly.

Instead of going up to the front door, he cut across waste ground at the back, vaulted the low garden fence and approached the kitchen window. His footsteps were muffled by snow as he crossed the back garden and crouched by the low window, peering in at his mother. Through a chink in the curtains he could see her laying the table for tea.

She still wore the same dark shawl about her shoulders,

still looked just as kindly and unflurried, though she seemed older, her shoulders thin and hunched. A clammy hand seized his heart: why hadn't he written more often, if only a few words?

She began frying two fish at the old stove; a loaf of bread, butter, two forks and plates, and a packet of salt stood on the table. Standing at the stove, her thin arms folded across her chest, she was lost in thought.

As he watched his mother through the window, he realized he could not possibly appear out of the blue; she might not survive the shock.

Right, then. He walked round to the front of the house and knocked firmly at the door. His mother's shaky voice echoed inside, asking who was there.

'Corporal Len Thwaites, South Riding Tank Corps,' he replied.

His heart was thumping so wildly he had to lean against the door post. No, she hadn't recognized his voice; he himself felt as if he was hearing it for the first time, so much had it altered after all the operations. It was low and husky.

'What dost tha want, lad?' she called.

'You're son, Lance-Corporal Clough, asked me to drop by while I'm on leave, like.'

She opened the door at once and grabbed his hands.

'Oh, come in, come on in, soldier,' she cried. 'How's my boy? I haven't had word in all but a year.'

He sat down at the kitchen table in the very chair where he had sat in the days before his legs were long enough to touch the floor; he recalled his mother patting his curly head and telling him to eat up or he wouldn't grow big and strong.

He started to talk about her son—about himself: what he ate and drank, the places he'd seen, how fit and well he was; he mentioned the tank battles only briefly.

'But doesn't war scare thee?' she asked, interrupting him, her eyes staring into his, yet focused elsewhere.

'Aye, it does that,' he said. 'But tha gits used to it.'

At that moment his father came in. He too had aged a lot; his hair and moustache looked as if they had been sprinkled with flour. He eyed the soldier, kicked the snow off his boots, slowly unwound his scarf, took off his donkey jacket and walked over to the table.

'Hey up, lad,' he said in greeting, shaking hands.

Ah, how well Terry knew that broad firm grip. Asking no questions—it was evident why this man in uniform was here—he sat down to listen with half-closed eyes.

The longer Terry sat there unrecognized, talking about himself as though he were someone else, the more impossible it was to reveal himself, to stand up and say, 'Don't you recognize me, Mam, Dad, disfigured though I am?'

Sitting there in his own cosy home, he felt both elated and desperately miserable.

'Right, mother, let's sup,' said Dad suddenly. 'Give t'lad my bloater, I'm not hungry.'

His father went over to the dresser. Yes, the matchbox full of fishhooks was still there, and the teapot with its chipped spout, and the dresser still smelt of cloves and bread crumbs. Two bottles of stout appeared on the table—with two glasses. This called for a celebration.

They all sat down to the meal, as in the old days. While they were eating, he noticed his mother following every movement of the hand in which he held his fork. He gave a nervous laugh, and she glanced away, her face creased in pain.

They talked of this and that, of the boys and old men conscripted for the pit, of the war and the letter from His Majesty the King to the Hateleys down the road. All at once, his mother asked, 'Tha hasn't said when our son'll get leave. We haven't set eyes on him for a couple of years. I expect he's a big strapping lad now, probably grown a moustache. And seeing death every day, as he does, I dare say his voice has changed, got rougher.'

'Aye, tha's reet,' he said. 'When he comes home tha mayst not recognize him.'

They made him a bed on the sofa. He remembered every fold and broken spring, every wallpaper pattern, every crack and line in the ceiling. The room smelt of warm bread and floor polish, of that homely comfort you never forget, even when you're facing death. The April wind whistled and murmured, rattling the window frames. Upstairs he could hear his father snoring gently; but his mother frequently sighed and stirred restlessly in her bed, she obviously could not sleep.

He lay still, covering his face with his hands.

'How could she not recognize me?'

In the morning he was woken by the crackle of burning wood and coal; his mother was quietly tending the fire. His socks, which she had washed, were hanging on a line strung across the kitchen; his boots had been polished and were standing by the door.

'Dost tha like jam butties?' she asked.

He didn't answer straight away. He swung his legs on to the floor, put on his shirt, trousers, and tunic, and sat there barefooted, staring at the lino.

'Does a Mary Casper still live in the village? John and Mabel Casper's lass?'

'She finished college last year,' said his mother. 'She's our schoolteacher now. Why, dost tha want to see lass?'

'Your son asked me to make sure I gave her his best wishes.'

His mother sent the little boy next door to fetch Mary. And before he had time to pull on his boots, Mary Casper was at the door. Her big grey eyes were shining, her dark brows raised in happy expectation, her cheeks flushed. When he saw her he almost groaned out loud: if only he could bury his face in that warm, dark hair.

This was exactly as he always pictured her: gentle and kind, flushed and lovely—so pretty the whole house seemed to glow the moment she entered.

'Have you brought news of Terry?' she enquired eagerly.

He was standing in the shadows, his back to the light; he merely nodded, unable to speak.

'Tell him I miss him heaps, I pray for him each night.'

She came closer. Her eyes met his and she fell back a pace, as though hit in the chest. The shock was written all over her face.

Straight away he made up his mind: he wouldn't stay a moment longer.

His mother made him some sandwiches for the journey. While she was cutting the bread, he talked again about Lance-Corporal Clough, this time about his brave deeds. He spoke roughly, his gaze fixed to the floor, so that he wouldn't see his ugliness reflected in Mary's eyes.

His father wanted to get a pit car to drive him to the station, but he went off alone on foot, as he had come.

He was so affected by what had happened that he kept stopping on the road, pressing his hands to his face and muttering hoarsely, 'My God! My God! What am I to do?'

He returned to his regiment, and got such a welcome from his comrades that it cheered him up somewhat, though he still found difficulty eating and sleeping. He had come to a decision: his mother need not know about his fate for the time being. As for Mary, he would pluck that thorn from his heart.

About a month later he received a letter from his mother.

Dear Son,

I'm so scared of writing; I scarcely know what to think. We had a visit from a soldier who said he had come on your behalf. He was a smashing lad, but his face was badly disfigured. Strange, he was going to stay with us for a while, but he changed his mind, and he up and left suddenly. And ever since, my son, I haven't been able to sleep at all— because I know that lad was you.

Your dad says I'm daft: 'If it'd been our son, he would've

said. Why should he do otherwise? A man should be proud to have a face like that.'

Dad did his best to convince me, but a mother's heart knows otherwise—it *was* my son, it *is* my son, it tells me.

The soldier slept on our sofa and I took his army coat out into the garden to clean it, and I held it close and wept because I knew it was yours.

Dear Terry, please, please, for my sake, write and tell me what's happened.

All our love,
Mum x x x x x x x

Well, to cut a long story short, Lance-Corporal Clough showed me the letter and, as he told me his story, he wiped his eyes on his sleeve. I told him straight, no messing, 'You stupid ha'po'th. Write to your mum at once, ask her to forgive you. A fat lot she cares what you look like! She'll love you even more as you are now.'

He did write. That same day.

Dear Mum and Dad,
I'm so sorry. Please forgive me. I was an idiot. It *was* me, your son Terry, who came to see you . . .

And so on, for another four pages, in small handwriting. He would have written twenty if he'd had the time.

It must have been about seven months later, the war over, that our troopship arrived at Southampton Docks. Terry and I were coming down the gangplank when this sailor at the bottom called up, 'Anyone here by the name of Lance-Corporal Clough?'

When Terry responded, the sailor said sternly, 'You're wanted, Lance-Corporal, over in the visitors' room beside the mess.'

Lance-Corporal Clough was clearly uneasy—he kept coughing and clearing his throat. I stayed a couple of paces back as he marched over to the room, knocked and went in.

I heard a woman's voice through the open door, 'Hello, Son, it's me.'

I saw a middle-aged woman clinging to him. And through the half-open door I could see a younger woman in the room. Well, I know we hadn't seen women for a while, but I've never clapped eyes on one prettier before or since.

He freed himself from his mother and turned to face this girl. As I said before, in his army uniform he stood tall and handsome, like a god of war.

'Mary,' he said, 'tha shouldn't have come. Tha promised to wait for another man, not me as I am now . . .'

It was too much to bear. But as I went to turn away, I heard her say, 'I'm going to live with you for ever and ever. I love you truly, with all my heart. Don't send me away.'

So there you are: it's not what's outside, it's what's inside a person that counts—the beauty of the human heart.

6
Unexpected Visitor

I read the story over and over again. And one day, when Hilary, my nosy neighbour, came in to take back her book, she asked me whether I had enjoyed the stories. As usual I ignored her—which came as no surprise to her. Yet as she was going through the door, she was suddenly halted by a voice behind her.

''Snot true, though. It couldn't happen in real life!'

She slowly turned round, her face a picture of shock and delight. She'd won at last. She stood there triumphantly, hands on hips, staring at me.

'You obviously didn't read the book very carefully, did you?' she said sarcastically. 'The back cover says they're all *true* stories.'

'Well, they would say that, wouldn't they!' I said moodily.

'So you don't believe people act like that in real life?' Her question was an obvious challenge.

'No, publishers will print anything to sell books,' I muttered. 'And anyway, a pretty girl wouldn't stick with someone as badly disfigured as that bloke in the story; 'tisn't natural.'

'Oh, so what's natural, clever clogs?' she said contemptuously. 'You've had great experience of life, you tell me.'

I could see through her ruse: if she got me mad she'd keep me talking. And I was so riled I couldn't resist.

'What's natural, what's human nature, is to feel disgust at a face like yours. Or mine, for that matter,' I hastily added, seeing the pain in her eyes.

That was below the belt, I knew it. But she wasn't going to play games with me and get away with it.

'If you don't believe it,' she said, tears starting in her eye slits, 'write to the publisher. Find out for yourself!'

With that she dropped the book on my bed and flounced out of the room.

'All right, I will,' I muttered when she'd gone. 'Stupid girl! Females will believe anything, they're so gullible.'

Determined to prove her wrong—though, to be honest, I was fascinated to discover the truth of the matter myself—I sat down later that day to write a letter. All I had was lined paper from my school exercise book; I tore out a page and started to write:

Dear Sir,

I've just read 'A Soldier's Tale' in your collection of stories of heroism in war. It's a good yarn, I enjoyed it. But things like that don't happen in real life. You see, I'm 'disfigured' too, so I know what I'm talking about.

Terry Clough's story has a happy ending; it's not believable. People aren't like that. They turn away from horror, freaks, scarred faces. It's wrong to feed people like us with false hope.

I signed the letter 'Master Billy Riley', folded the page and squeezed it into a buff envelope from my bedside drawer. Gran was due later in the week and she could put a tuppeny-ha'penny stamp on and post it for me.

Several weeks later, our happy-go-lucky odd-job man, Harry, approached me in the breakfast hall with a big bright beam on his wizened face.

'Now, young fellow-me-lad,' he said breezily, 'I've a letter for you.'

He held it out in front of his nose as if it was a bouquet of roses.

'For Master Billy Riley,' he read on the envelope, sniffing it as if the smell would reveal the sender's identity.

'Maybe it's some rich widow who's fallen in love with a handsome young chap like you?' he said happily.

'Give it here,' I muttered irritably.

Who on earth was writing to me? I'd forgotten all about my letter to the publisher. The other kids round the table craned their necks to take a peek at the contents as I cut open the envelope with a knife. I told them it was private and confidential, shielding the long creamy page from idle gazers.

In fact, the typed message was brief.

Dear Master Riley,

Thank you for your communication of the tenth of June. Its contents have been noted and sent on to the man in the story you allude to.

Yours sincerely,
Clive Larkin
Managing Editor

That was it. No confirmation. No denial of fact or fiction. I didn't know what 'allude' meant, but it made no difference. I clearly had embarrassed the publishers, caught them with their pants down; they were seeking to blind me with big words so that I wouldn't accuse them of fraud.

The letter spoke for itself. I received no further long white envelopes. All the same, I felt slightly more pally towards haughty Hilary—which meant I didn't bang on her wall quite so often when she played her wind-up gramophone or switched on her wireless. I felt that I now had the upper hand, and had proved what a silly goose she was.

One day soon after I slipped the creamy page under her door. I heard no more about it, and she stopped coming to see me. I was sorry about her cutting off my supply of goodies, but I didn't miss the company.

It must have been about six weeks later, one rainy Sunday afternoon in August when it was too wet to go out for a walk in the woods. I was sitting alone in the conservatory, reading the *Wizard*. All of a sudden, matron came in with a tall, fair-haired man in a raincoat. I'd never seen him before. He looked a bit holier than thou, as if he was from the Salvation Army; or maybe he was the local beadle come to punish me for skipping classes.

'This is our Billy,' said matron in her usual matter-of-fact tone.

When she went out, the man thanked her in an odd accent as she took his wet hat and coat. He was left holding a khaki bag in his hands, like an army rucksack: he put it gently on the floor before drawing up a wicker chair and sitting down beside me.

'Hello, Billy, lad.'

For the first time I noticed his scars. In an institution like ours, you get used to disfigured faces; perhaps that's why I hadn't noticed the blotches and rugged lines of his features. Or maybe it was because he held himself so surely, so upright, as if the lack of a human face didn't matter to him. Most of us slouched, drawing our heads into our shoulders, trying to conceal our faces.

I nodded, biding my time, waiting to find out who he was.

'How's tha doin', lad?'

Was this some psychiatrist sent to prise open a misery-guts like me? Then I suddenly realized: he must be a soldier from Dad's regiment come to describe his last moments of glory. Well, his smile might charm the birds down from the trees, but it made me even more wary. I needed proof of his identity.

'I hear tha's at odds with t'world,' he said in his funny sing-song accent. 'Quite reet too, lad, quite reet. I felt t'same first off; it's natural enough. You lose your faith in folk, hate thissen and others, just want to crawl away and hide in a dark hole.'

That was about it. He'd put his finger on it—it was

refreshing to hear the truth and not be fed on 'Cheer up, old son, worse things happen at sea . . . ' 'You'll soon be looking grand, keep your pecker up!' This bloke had clearly been through the mill himself by the look of him. But who was he?

It wasn't long before the penny dropped.

'I've come a long way to see thee, Billy,' he said with a sigh, 'and I haven't got long before my train returns. Look, son, I got thy letter from publisher. And I had a note from a mate of thissen, a nice lass, someone who cares about thee. She thought it might do thee good to hear t'truth at first hand.'

I stared hard in astonishment. It was as if Dick Barton had entered the room when you know he doesn't exist. Surely not. Terry? Terry Clough?

My lips must have formed the words, for the man gave me a warm smile as he nodded. But the shock must have stung my vocal chords because sounds now began to tumble out.

'Jiminy Cricket! But you're only in a story.' He looked taken aback, so I quickly added, 'I'm a bit lost for words. This is a shock . . . '

'That's understandable,' he said seriously, extending a scarred, patchy brown-white hand.

Slowly I took it in both my hands, overcome with excitement.

He had come all this way to see *me*! Here, sitting beside me was the real-life soldier who had gone through all those terrible trials I'd read about. My hero. I owed Hilary an apology. Whether I'd give it or not was another matter. So the cunning little vixen had written too—trying to help. Well, you could knock me down with a feather!

As he slackened his grip, I realized all at once that both my hands were hurting badly—I hadn't shaken hands since before the bomb. It must have been painful for him too, for I noticed him wince.

'Sorry, lad,' he muttered. 'My mitts are still tender where the tendons snapped. Even now I can't do daft things like tie up shoelaces or fasten buttons.'

He gave a throaty laugh, which reminded me of the time his mum and dad hadn't recognized his voice. At least my squeaky voice hadn't changed.

'Life's tough, son,' he continued. 'But you'll find plenty less fortunate than us—some are blind, some have no arms or legs, some are paralysed from the neck down. Think how humiliating that is, allus depending on someone else, nobut chained to a wheelchair or a bed.'

Funny, up till then, I hadn't really given it a thought. He was right. At least I was free to eat or not, walk down the passage or not, lock myself in my room . . . or not.

He broke into my musings.

'At least thee and me, we can see and smell a beautiful spring day, hear the birds chirruping in the trees, a kitten miaowing, a girl's words of love. We can walk through a field of daisies and breathe in the heady smell of new-mown hay. And, son, most importantly, thee and me, we can talk to each other.' He leaned closer and spoke earnestly, 'Don't deny thissen nature's greatest gift, something the animals can't do.'

By this time I was hanging on his every word. But I had to ask him *the* question, however painful the answer might be. To him, and to me.

'Excuse me asking, but there's one question I must know the answer to.'

'Get on, then,' he said with a smile. 'Words aren't as painful as burns.'

I swallowed hard, then forced out the words with breaking voice, 'Are you still with Mary?'

He rocked back in his chair, his long fair hair bobbing up and down; and he let out a peal of merry laughter that must have echoed through the whole house on this drab empty Sunday afternoon.

'Billy, Billy, what a question! She's as loving and adorable as ever. We had a wonderful wedding. Now we have a baby son, a lovely wee fellow. We couldn't be happier. It's two years now since we tied the knot. We've our own council house, Mary's left her teaching job to look after our Joey, and I'm working as a union official at t'pit; it doesn't pay too grand, but we manage.'

I asked him more questions—about his mother and father, about the tank driver who'd saved his life. Did people in his village stare at him, whisper behind his back, go out of their way to avoid him? Did kids call him names?

He answered patiently, and the afternoon passed. All at once, he glanced at his watch in alarm.

'By gum, look at t'time. I'll miss my train if I don't rush. Oh and by the way, one last thing. I play trombone in our colliery band; I find music a great boon: it's a good equalizer and helps thee forget tha worries. Here, I've a little present for thee: my dad gave me it.'

Fishing into his bag on the floor, he pulled out a long black and silver instrument and handed it over as if it were a crystal goblet.

'Learn to play, Billy. Express thissen in music. Show people what tha can do. And don't forget: it's not what's on the outside, it's what's on the inside that counts.'

We shook hands, gently this time, and he was gone before I had time to thank him properly. I was not to know then the true worth of his gift.

7
Confidence

It was now four years since the bomb had nosedived into my life and just over three years that I had been locked away in this home for the unsightly. Not that I wanted to escape from my sanctuary. The home *was* my home, I had nowhere else to go; the idea of walking down the street and being stared at frightened me silly.

'Hey, Mum, look at that monster! It must have escaped from the loony bin.'

I was certain outsiders would think I was wrong in the head as well as the face.

Once, on one of my regular 'face adjustment' trips to the town hospital, our van drew up at a red light. I was sitting next to the driver as a car stopped alongside us; and this spotty boy of about my age started poking faces at me through the window. When I pressed my faceless face against the glass, he got the shock of his life. He looked as if he had just seen a ghost, turning green, amber, and red, in tune with the changing traffic lights. I'm sure my horror mask haunted him for months afterwards. He probably never pulled a face again, fearing he would be stuck like that forever!

My visits to the special burns unit were now less frequent, about every two or three months. Good old 'Whitewash', as I called the plastic surgeon Mr Whiteway, had sliced off every spare piece of flesh on my body to graft on to my hands, arms, and face. The idea, he said, was to remove wafers of living skin from my thighs, shoulders, and especially my bottom, for planting elsewhere.

The machine he used reminded me of the bacon slicer they had on the Co-op counter; and I was the porker being sliced up for dinner, except that my patches were then sewn on to my own parts. I was being re-covered and re-fashioned like an old armchair.

It was a lengthy process, and not all progress. We sort of zigzagged—sometimes the skin didn't take, like planting seeds that don't come up; sometimes it turned from blushing pink to blotchy brown, like flaked-off tree-trunk bark.

No longer did I scrutinize my features every day in my little face mirror; it was all too depressing. There were times when I gave up hope altogether and retreated into myself. Who would think I'd hurt so deeply? It wasn't just feeling sorry for myself; it was the terrible memories and nightmares.

I felt that someone had cheated me; and that made me angry. The worst thing was that I didn't know who to blame. So I blamed everybody, the whole world, myself included. *Especially myself.*

Sometimes I thought the reflection could not possibly be mine; it *must* be someone else since I didn't recognize anything of my former self. After seeing the Disney film *Snow White and the Seven Dwarfs*, I became fascinated with the scene where the Wicked Queen gazes at herself in the mirror. It reminded me of my own routine dekko at the oracle. Only I had my own chant,

> 'Mirror, mirror on the wall,
> Who is the ugliest of them all?'

And the mirror would reply,

> 'You, O Billy, are very ugly,
> But Hilary who lives next door
> Is uglier by far!'

Ha-ha! Sometimes the mirror would answer Ted or matron or Hazel or Donald, whoever happened to be in my bad books. That used to cheer me up a whisker. Instead of having pity for my fellow inmates, it was a relief to think there were some ghastlier than me. True, matron wasn't disfigured, she was just plain ugly.

Old 'Whitewash' had most trouble getting my eyes and nose right. From the start I needed special drops because my eyes were constantly stretching open till it hurt; the eyelids used to puff up and then shrink, and I found it impossible to blink. Finally, 'Whitewash' decided to carry out some emergency repairs to get the lids blinking.

Thankfully, it worked a treat and I never had trouble opening and closing my eyes again. But that was a rare victory. Mind you, I still looked like the panda in Chessington Zoo, with white eyes in the middle of a red face and a funny upturned button of a nose.

The skin from my backside grafted on to my nose also kept shrinking, so pulling the tip of my nose upwards. I began to resemble Pinocchio: I even imagined it was because I told the occasional fib that my nose tipped upwards. So I used to go through the day determined not to talk, which made me even surlier than ever.

Yet my bum-nose still cocked a snoot at me.

On my regular hospital visits 'Whitewash' would click and cluck like an old cock linnet, chattering away to himself, 'Oh, bother and blow, bother and blow. Must do deeper dermals here, a split-skin graft there . . . '

I never knew what he was on about; we talked a different language altogether. He was stiff and awkward with words—I put it down to his posh public school upbringing, forever going on about 'surgical adjustments, recuperation, series of operations. It'll take a few years before we sort it out, old fellow.'

A few years! I certainly would be an 'old fellow' by then.

He saw that the slow process was getting me down. So one day he said he wanted to have a man-to-man talk with me. What on earth was coming? Perhaps he was going to tell me about the birds and the bees; not that I needed such knowledge in my monkish state.

'Look, Billy, we've come a long way in the three years and a bit since we started all this. I think it's high time we thought about where we're heading.'

He drew a deep breath and looked obviously ill at ease. I realized that old 'Whitewash', who had spent so much time trying to help me, was much better with his hands than his words. Poor old boy, he was doing his best to mend my mind as well as my body.

'I know you wish you weren't scarred, you dream of having your old face back, having clean, smooth hands. But dreams and wishful thinking exist only under the skin. It's in the real world we have to live.'

He could see by my eyes that he had struck a chord and had my attention. I like someone who gives it to me straight, far better than 'You'll be fine one day'. I even wished I could help this timid, modest genius who was doing his damndest to get the message over.

'You must accept that you're disfigured. And you're going to stay disfigured. You won't wake up with the body beautiful tomorrow. You're *never* going to wake up and find the scars have all gone. Of course, you'll improve with time, but the disfigurement will never go away. Am I making myself clear?'

I nodded glumly. He clearly needed reassurance that his words were seeping through my thick skull.

'That doesn't stop you from being a human being, it doesn't stop you from being accepted, from getting a job, from falling in love one day, getting married, having a family . . . doing all the other things that make life worthwhile.'

I must have screwed up my nose at the very idea of having a girlfriend, let alone getting married. At fifteen and a bit I was beginning to think of girls, even the sad excuses for females that slouched around our home. Yet every time my thoughts strayed in that direction I felt revulsion at myself. What decent girl in her right mind would fancy an eyesore like me?

'Don't spend all your time thinking of yourself,' the surgeon continued. 'Take a look at others—there are plenty worse off than you—and think what they've achieved. Ask yourself, why can't I do the same? What's so different about me that I can't do that? You've no excuse for not trying.'

I had to admit in my heart of hearts that old 'Whitewash' was right. He made me reflect on Terry Clough's life. After all, Terry was even less of an oil painting than I was, yet he'd got himself a job, a house, a wife and kid; most of all he had confidence. He lost it, found it, then built it up, believed in it and gave it to others.

Could I do the same? I still doubted it.

'If you've got confidence in yourself, people will accept you for what you are, what you can do. Be yourself, have faith in yourself and your abilities, and it'll work, you'll see. The only way we can get you accepted back into society is for you to get out there and live your life to the full.'

He paused before speaking again, this time less kindly, 'You can't do that by shutting yourself away in a darkened room, feeling sorry for yourself. Well, laddie?'

He deserved some sort of answer, if not a promise. Looking up at his anxious face, I felt a mixture of gratitude and amusement. His red forehead was speckled with grey droplets of sweat, his bushy eyebrows were hoisted half an inch closer to his silver hairline and his beaky freckled nose kept twitching like a rabbit's.

In other circumstances, I might have burst out laughing. Instead, I surprised him by smiling warmly.

'Thank you, sir,' I said. 'I'll try.'

8
The Clarinet

Had I heard the clarinet before? Possibly. I might have caught it in a dance band number or some orchestral concert. But I certainly wasn't aware of it. Hilary's wireless blared out music all day long, so I got my full ration of every instrument in the land, from tin whistle to castanets. As for Terry Clough's clarinet, I wasn't even sure which end you blew into.

My initial efforts did not enlighten me. It hadn't come with a 'How to Play' manual, so I didn't know how to get a note out of the darn thing. I tried blowing down one end and heard a rush of wind and a few squeals come out the other—like mice under the floorboards. I tried sucking and blowing raspberries, but nothing came of that either.

My musical efforts had to come in short bursts. Not through lack of interest or application; it was just that my mouth, throat, and lungs all ached from this blow-suck-blow activity. They all ganged up to deny me success; for a few days afterwards I found swallowing painful and my vocal chords twanged hoarsely.

Right, if they wanted a fight they could have it. A bit of discomfort wasn't going to put me off my music. And even if the novelty speedily wore off, I had another reason for persevering. My squeaky sound waves were penetrating the flimsy wall separating me from my noisy nuisance of a neighbour. Now it was her turn to cover her ears.

Sweet revenge. Or, in my case, honking, blasting, wailing revenge. It took no more than a couple of sessions for nosy Hilary to come to investigate the source of this infernal din.

Just as I was exploring the high and low notes one evening—bang, bang, bang on the door. In reply I played two notes, one high, one low:

'Come . . . innn.'

Mind you, it could just as easily have been 'Push . . . off.'

Quietly the door opened and Hilary entered, sitting down without a word on the edge of my bed. I half hoped she would be tearing her hair out, blue in the face, ranting and raving. But she wasn't. She sat there, hands folded in her lap, as meek as a lamb. After a while, she whispered reverently, as if in church, 'Do you mind if I listen?'

'You can do that in your own room,' was my unfriendly retort.

'I could,' she said after a pause. 'Or I could have drowned it out by turning up my wireless. But I wanted to see you play.'

That took the wind out of my sails. But I was still savouring my noisy revenge.

'Anyway, if I do disturb you it's your fault,' I muttered.

She took offence at last.

'Why are you always blaming others? How can it be my fault if you squeak and squawk?'

'You were the one who went and wrote to that soldier! He gave me the clarinet, so there!'

Her lidless panda eyes widened. Although word had quickly spread about my visitor—you couldn't keep any secret in this house of busybodies—she was still stunned by my having met Terry Clough. We hadn't exchanged a word since the visit; but now she could not contain herself.

'Oh, what's he like? Is he as handsome as in the book? How bad are his scars? Did he marry her? What did you talk about?'

I thought it only fair to answer as best I could. After

all, if it hadn't been for Hilary I wouldn't have known about the war hero, let alone actually met him in the flesh. And then there was the clarinet.

It was the first friendly chat we'd had. My clarinet turned out to be a pipe of peace. Or, rather, music had thawed the icicles of my frosty heart. True, I did owe her a good deal, far more even than I realized at the time.

'So there we are,' I said at last. 'I suppose I'd better say thanks . . . and sorry for being a Doubting Thomas.'

Having got that off my chest, I picked up the clarinet from the bedside table and said in a matter-of-fact tone, 'Now, if you don't mind, I've got to practise.'

'Of course,' she said blushing. 'May I listen for a bit?'

To her I now represented the war hero himself; a new respect shone in her eyes. I had met him, talked to him, shaken his hand, and he had given me new-found hope with this piece of shiny metal and black wood. My music was like the war hero's voice to Hilary.

From then on she would drop in regularly, sitting on my bed, listening quietly, watching my attempts to wring a tune from this stubborn stick of liquorice. When I tired of playing, I'd sometimes pop into her room to chat, borrow a book or comic, listen to *ITMA* or *Monday Night at Eight* and other radio comedy programmes. Best of all, she let me play a record on her gramophone.

Hilary had a well-to-do aunty who used to come to see her once a week; she'd bring her a few knick-knacks, books, and even new records. I noticed that the record collection now began to include clarinet music—all sorts, from the jazz of Sidney Bechet and Artie Shaw to big band swing, bebop, and popular tunes of the day. And she had one classical record: Mozart's Clarinet Concerto.

I'd never really listened to classical music before; I thought it was only for toffs. Yet while I soon got bored with jazz and pop tunes, I never tired of listening to

Mozart, finding something new every time. Although it was extraordinarily hard to play, I made big efforts to learn bits of it by heart.

Now and then, Hilary would let me borrow her gramophone, and I would carry it carefully into my room, set it down on my table, take the Mozart from its brown sleeve, wind up the machine and stand there, clarinet at the ready. It wasn't easy because I had to crank the handle of the gramophone every few minutes as the music slowed to a low whine before gathering pace again:

Dum-dum-dum . . . Dummmm, dummmmmmm, dummmmmm . . . Dum-dum-dum.

Then, after several playings, I'd have to change the needle in the head as the record went scratchy. I played it over and over and over again until I almost knew it off by heart. I would hum the orchestral introduction and the breaks in the middle, beating time with my hand until the clarinet came in; then I'd try desperately to keep up with the music. At first, I could manage only the slow parts, with more squeaky fluffs than trills. But steadily I got to grips with the rest, not as fast as on the record, more at my own pace, as the gramophone wound down.

There can't be many clarinettists whose first piece of music was Mozart—like cooking a six-course banquet before you've even made a bowl of porridge.

And I made another discovery. It wasn't enough just to master the tune; there was so much more to it— beating time with my foot so as to play evenly, playing softly, mellowly, sweetly in the slow parts, loudly and strongly in others.

There was more to this music lark than I'd bargained for.

After a couple of months my lips and throat were strong enough to get through a session without too much pain; but my lungs always let me know their dislike of music. I was quite used to pain by now and knew that I would never achieve anything without suffering agony. So be it. It was either surrender or fight on. And I was stubborn. If Terry Clough could win, so could I.

Now, every so often the nutcases in our madhouse used to put on little concerts in the ballroom; it still had a stage at one end, presumably where the band used to play in the good old balmy pre-war days. I could just picture the ballroom stuffed with young blades all togged up in white tie and tails, whirling their bejewelled debs round the shiny parquet floor or prancing about in the Charleston.

Up till now I had never gone along to these 'freak shows' as I called them, preferring my own company, head buried in my own world of adventure comic strips. But Christmas was coming and lots of relatives and bigwigs had been invited to our Christmas concert. The 'Ringmaster', as he was known, was our Ted, a cheery rosy-cheeked fellow with no chin or hair, which made him look like a body with a round apple on top—rather like William Tell's son with the apple but no head.

Although Ted could only grunt, we all understood him since he'd wave and shrug until he got his message through. I never knew anyone who could speak so clearly with his body. Ted was almost twenty and had been in the Home from the beginning of the war. He tried life on the outside, but soon returned, begging for a job; and they had taken him on as gardener. Besides tending the lawns and flowers, he grew all manner of vegetables and fruit, from radishes and potatoes to rhubarb and gooseberries, in the back garden.

Oddly, this hearty outdoor type with hands as rough and earthy as his potato patch, possessed an uncommon talent: he played the violin. He was always saying that the plants and trees were living beings who understood music; and they would sing and natter to him in return.

He'd walk through the gardens and woods in all weathers, playing his fiddle and crooning to Mother Nature.

I think the animals and insects must have taken a shine to his playing too because he was forever cursing the slugs and caterpillars that ate his cabbages and lettuces, and the moles and foxes who played havoc with his lawn.

Ted had evidently got to hear of my clarinet playing and was delighted to find a soul-mate. So he invited me to audition for a slot in the Christmas programme. The Ringmaster must have liked what he'd heard—or maybe he was scraping the barrel for artists—since he asked me not only to play a couple of Christmassy songs, but to do a duet with him.

I suggested the Mozart, which he accepted rather grudgingly—since it was more clarinet than violin. Anyway, he did have his own solo spot in which he gave a rendition of 'In a Monastery Garden', which was fairly apt since the garden was normally his stage.

Ted also directed us kids in scenes from *Snow White and the Seven Dwarfs*. Hilary, of course, was Snow White, and Dorothy, a very pretty older girl with one arm and no legs, was the Wicked Queen. In our scale of values, it seemed right to have an ugly Snow White and a pretty witch. My role was Grumpy, which I didn't mind, remembering how grumpy I had been for the past three years. As Ted said, 'It didn't take much acting from me.' At least he didn't make me Dopey—that part went to the youngest boy, Donald, who had cauliflower ears and no nose.

For about a month we spent much of our spare time preparing for the big event—painting scenery, making costumes out of old clothes someone had unearthed in the attic, rehearsing our lines and generally fooling about. At least the concert helped us forget our private woes.

Ted and I did our duetting in a little grove of silver birch trees. It was a hard slog learning the part and usually pretty chilly, aggravating my already wheezy chest. But I've never worked so happily at any task as I did at getting my contribution right. I had never imagined how wonderful it was to play in the open air, with blue skies above and birds singing in the trees. The notes seem to sprout wings, swooping through the air and soaring up into the sky until all the heavens sang.

'Silent Night' was certainly not silent, and 'Jingle Bells' was never so jingly. But it was Mozart that thrilled me most, perhaps because we were making music together, or simply because we had to work so hard to get it right.

Ted and I loved our music-making. But would others? We were soon to find out.

9
Christmas Concert

At last the day of the concert dawned. I spent most of the morning and early afternoon going over and over my songs and concert piece. At about five o'clock the guests started to arrive. You might have thought they'd come for a stately ball: most of the women were decked out in gowns and glittering necklaces, while the men had come as penguins—all white tie and tails and shiny black shoes.

Gran and Sis arrived late. We had arranged tea and cakes in the drawing room, each 'family' assigned to a set of chairs and little round table. The idea was for us hosts to greet our visitors and have a little chinwag before the concert—or, in Ted's case, an arm and leg wag.

Iris had brought a young man I'd never met before.

'My fiancé, Fred,' she said by way of introduction.

He didn't seem too comfortable at meeting Iris's 'skeleton in the cupboard', her ugly brother.

'So you're Billy,' he said, shaking hands. 'I've heard a lot about you.'

I bet he had: all bad. He tried to be chatty, but the look in his eyes betrayed his awkwardness. Who could blame him? Apart from doctors, I've yet to meet someone for the first time without seeing a forced, embarrassed smile on their pained faces.

Gran was looking quite old and frail, but she put on a brave face, saying how proud she was of me.

'Och, who'd have thought! Our Willie a musician. Begorrah, it's the Irish in you, me boy.'

That said, she was unusually quiet. It was Iris who did most of the talking—and eating. She must have scoffed half a dozen of Hilary's fairy cakes. Fred just nibbled a jam tart and seemed relieved when I made my excuses to go and get changed into my Grumpy outfit.

The first half of our concert was *Snow White*—where she stumbles upon the little cottage deep in the woods, meets the seven dwarfs, and is poisoned by the wicked witch. It ended with her being saved by the Handsome Prince or, in our case, Gruesome Ted the gardener.

I don't think the audience knew whether to laugh or cry. Still, even though Happy and Doc forgot half their lines and no one could make out Ted's words, it earned warm applause—probably relief that it was all over.

I was first on after the interval, playing my two songs. I had never played in public before and the prospect scared me stiff. It's one thing serenading the birds, it's quite another standing on a spotlit stage peering out into the dark and glimpsing row upon row of shadowy faces. I couldn't spot Gran or Sis in the grey void. Since it was our Ringmaster who had to introduce me, the audience was none the wiser whether this was *Snow White* again: Grumpy and his Clarinet.

I was shaking like a leaf as I put the clarinet to my lips. Since I couldn't read a note of music, I wasn't able to hide behind a music stand; I played by ear. My throat and lips were as dry as a bone and I felt a sharp pain in my chest even before I'd applied for puff.

The dreaded disaster happened. My clarinet let out a strangled squawk, like a hungry gannet.

The disgust I felt at myself helped me overcome my nerves. Out of the corner of my eye I could see Ted flapping in the wings: he was a bigger bag of nerves than me.

'Right, Billy, you prat,' I told myself angrily, 'don't you dare let Gran down!'

Slowly I lowered the clarinet, wiped my sweaty hands on my trousers, licked my lips, then put the instrument to my mouth once more. I got through 'Silent Night' without a hitch and was just about to launch into 'Jingle Bells' when a strange thing happened.

Someone at the back started clapping. And Gran's voice rang distinctly in my ears, 'Lovely, Willie, just lovely.'

Then the entire audience started clapping, and someone shouted 'Bravo!'

I wasn't sure what 'Bravo' meant, but I assumed they wanted a second tune—the only other one I knew. So this time I gave them 'Jingle Bells'. Being carried away with the first success, I went too fast for my own good and fluffed a few notes. Even so, they clapped again for a full minute.

I bowed and scuttled off stage. Ted was beaming.

'Well done, maestro,' he grunted.

As songs and poems kept the audience occupied, I went backstage to put out the fire in my chest with a glass of cream soda. And to reflect.

'Well, well, Billy boy, you did it! Now don't go getting too cocky, you've got the Mozart yet—that'll bore the pants off them. Mustn't let Ted down though.'

After wetting my whistle, I hurried off to my room for last minute practice. Our duet was the last item on the programme—'Keeping the best till last,' as Ted had said in his modest way. I trilled up and down the scales, then ran through parts of the piece calmly and far too fast. Still, satisfied I'd done all I could, I walked slowly back to the ballroom and slipped behind the curtain into the wings.

Dorothy was on stage in her wheelchair, reciting in her strong Cornish accent, 'Old Meg she were a Gypsy and lived upon the moors . . . '

After a polite round of applause, she cycled herself into the wings to make way for Ted. He was wearing a nifty, if shabby, black dinner jacket which I'd last seen on the orchard scarecrow. But Ted had cleaned and patched it up, and from a distance it looked reasonably respectable.

'Now, ladies and gentlemen, our final number—some serious music, featuring Billy Riley on clarinet and yours truly on violin.'

Whether the audience understood or not goodness only knows; but our purpose was clear when Ted picked up his violin from a chair at the side of the stage and I stepped into the spotlight with my clarinet.

We were both used to playing standing up in the woods, as we serenaded the rooks and woodpigeons. Now we stood opposite each other at the front of the stage, composing ourselves for the duet. I didn't feel so nervous this time. If anything, I had to concentrate hard and try to avoid looking at Ted: every time I saw him with the violin stuck under his chinless face I felt an attack of the giggles coming on. He looked so comical in his oversized dinner jacket, with his billiard ball head and a happy grin on his rosy-cheeked face.

Fortunately, Ted had a couple of minutes solo before I came in, and the moment the Concerto started I blotted all else out of my mind and felt completely at one with the music. So when I started to play, I was carried away by the sheer beauty of it all. No doubt, my performance was pretty amateurish to those listening and I missed a few high notes; my pianissimos were too fortissimo, and my glissandos were often in danger of sliding off the register altogether. But we got through it without any major mishap.

In the lull that followed our finale I suddenly realized how utterly drained I was. And soaking wet.

The silence did not last long; it was broken by frantic clapping which went on for several minutes and was interspersed with shouts of 'Bravo, bravo, bravissimo!' I doubt whether Mozart himself ever enjoyed greater acclaim than Ted and I did that December evening in 1947.

But we soon came down to earth with a bump when they called for an encore. We didn't know any more!

After bowing for the umpteenth time, we stood still as a powdered lady in a flowery frock climbed the steps to the stage with two bouquets of red roses in her arms. She presented one to Ted and one to me, then planted a kiss on our cheeks. I noticed Ted peering suspiciously at the blooms, no doubt wondering whether someone had pinched his precious Christmas roses from the garden. Looking at Ted's mournful expression, I just had to let myself go in a great burst of laughter.

Only then did I feel a searing pain in my chest, and I collapsed in a fit of coughing. Ted helped me off the stage while the powdery lady addressed the audience, thanking them for coming, paying tribute to staff and patients for all their wonderful efforts, explaining how much it cost to run the home, the value of music in helping to prepare the less fortunate (that was us!) for the outside world. Blah, blah, blah.

When Gran, Sis, and Fred came to my room to say goodbye, I was already tucked up in bed, still wheezing from my exertions. For the first time in my life I noticed genuine tears of joy and pride in my sister's eyes—though I'd seen plenty of tears of rage in the past! Gran just grinned from ear to ear. As for Fred, he was still awkward in my company, but there was a new gleam of admiration in his eyes.

'Thanks, Billy,' he said. 'To be frank, I thought I'd find it tough getting through this evening. But I really enjoyed it thanks to you. You've a rare talent, kiddo. Use it.'

'I always knew he had it in him,' murmured Gran.

Sis couldn't speak at all. She just blubbered.

They shuffled out and I lay back exhausted on the pillow. Beside me under the covers I lovingly clutched my clarinet.

'Thanks, Terry,' I whispered.

10
Presents

On Christmas morning after breakfast I joined the
throng around the big Christmas tree in the ballroom.
Ted had kindly donated one of the fir trees on 'his'
estate, though it took much begging and bullying to get
it out of him.

Mind you, he must have picked the mankiest tree in
the woods since it had sparse brown branches and a bald
head, just like Ted. We did our best to cover its blushes
with silver tinsel, a paper angel on top, and pink, blue,
and yellow paper chains we'd glued together ourselves.
And out of the cupboard beneath the stairs came the
once-a-year fairy lights that had certainly seen better
days; half the bulbs were missing. To save electricity
matron only let us switch them on for an hour on
Christmas Eve and Christmas morning.

I had already received some presents—five Christmas
cards. Since I never had any letters, apart from the
publisher's that time, it was a welcome treat, particularly
as they each came on separate days. Two cards were
from Gran and Iris, and there was a nice card with a
family photograph from the Clough family—Terry,
Mary, and Joey—who all sent their love and best
wishes. Two cards had old stamps glued on the
envelopes, so I knew they hadn't come through the
post. One was a snowy woodland scene with the
message: 'To my fellow musician, Billy the Blow, from
Fiddler Ted.' The other said simply, 'To my best
friend, Billy, Happy Xmas. Love, Hilary.'

That warmed me no end. I didn't mind the 'Love' bit,
but I did feel bad that I hadn't sent her a card. Since I
had no money, I hadn't sent anyone a real card. Come to

think of it, I hardly knew what pounds, shillings, and pence were apart from in my maths books.

I never had to buy any necessities: the comics and clothes came free, second hand from charities. Books and records I borrowed from my pals, and such luxuries as sweets and biscuits came mainly from Hilary and her kindly aunt. One thing about the home was that those more fortunate in receiving parcels and presents normally shared out any goodies with the rest of us.

So there we were, all standing around, chatting, pretending we didn't know what was coming next, when the doors burst open with a clatter and in came a red-cloaked figure with a long white fluffy cotton beard; over one shoulder was a bulging brown sack—one of Ted's old spud sacks by the look and smell of it.

We could all see the brown boots of handyman Harry poking out from under the cloak hem, and we recognized his husky voice as he did his best to give a Christmassy 'Ho-ho-ho' chortle. As he reached the tree, Harry Christmas untied his sack and started to call out the names on the parcels. Since his reading skills weren't so polished, matron stood at his shoulder ready to help him out on the longer names.

My name was called three times. Surprise! Surprise! I expected only two presents. But Christmas always throws up surprises. The first parcel contained some sweets and nuts and my usual *Boy's Own Annual*. Gran, of course. But the gift from Iris and Fred was unexpected. It felt solid and heavy, and turned out to be an illustrated book on the life of Wolfgang Amadeus Mozart. I was delighted. Good old Sis, or was it Fred?

As for the third parcel, I couldn't make it out. I had no more relatives, and certainly no wealthy friends on the outside. The brown paper wrapping looked and smelt posh and expensive, and the writing on the cover was bold and unfamiliar: 'To Master W. Riley. Not to be opened till Christmas.' It had obviously come by post since the king's head was smudged by a purple stamp. The packet was wide and flat—a set of old comics? Most welcome.

I was to be disappointed.

As I tore open the brown paper and untied the twine, I found a big black and white book with several white sheets of paper underneath; they all bore different names and pictures: 'Paper Doll', 'The Gypsy', 'Coming Round the Mountain', 'So Tired', 'Trees'.

The book's front cover had just two words in big print:

CLARINET PRIMER

Seeing my look of disappointment, Ted put his arm round my shoulders, saying, 'You lucky beggar! That's worth a thousand comics. Now you can learn to read music and play any piece you want. Gosh, how I wish I could read music.'

He was right when I came to think about it. What use was a comic once you'd read it, except for swaps? But if I could read music and learn to play properly, there was no limit to what I could do. After all, if ever I wanted to play in a band—dance, brass, jazz, Palm Court—I would have to learn my part and follow the conductor's instructions.

That instruction manual turned out to be the most useful present I'd ever received. For a start I learned a valuable tip that saved me a lot of chest ache: how to breathe through my nose while playing and not have to take great gulps of air. That took the strain off my lungs, though the pain never went altogether.

Every spare moment in the Christmas holidays I spent poring over my primer and turning words and squiggles into musical sounds. I decided not to play another tune until I had learned the basics, taught myself to read music; the hardest thing of all was to undo the bad habits I had acquired; that took a deal of patience and repetition. Hilary must have been blasted out of her mind; yet she never complained.

Once I got the hang of it I even tried writing some simple melodies myself, and I gave the resident cat the benefit of a première performance of 'Sadhouse Blues' by William Riley. We formed a duet: she sang the tune while I accompanied her on the clarinet. I don't think she liked the arrangement too much because she fled into the barn every time she saw me approaching, clarinet or no clarinet.

About a month later I received my second ever letter. This time it was from someone I'd never heard of: a Mr Alexander Maisky. The message on a white card inside the envelope was formal and brief:

> Mr and Mrs Maisky request the pleasure
> of your company at a musical recital on
> Sunday 10 March at 2 p.m.

There followed a personal note to me,

Dear Master Riley,
                          Please bring your clarinet and prepare
a short performance: something light and breezy perhaps.
                    A car will collect you at 12.45.
                              Yours,
                                    Alexander Maisky

The address was in the nearby town, about fifteen miles away. It must be one of those snooty places because it had a name, Fidelio, rather than a number.

Well, well! I was puzzled by the invitation, especially when I discovered that Ted wasn't on the visiting list. Yet the more I thought about it, the more I got cold feet. It dawned on me that I'd never left the home in all my nearly four years here, apart from hospital visits.

I also used to go walking in the woods, always keeping off the beaten track. There were times when the devil got into me and I longed to jump out on some passer-by with a 'BOO!', then run away. But I couldn't be that cruel—I might give some poor soul a heart attack!

I knew I'd have to leave the home soon after my seventeenth birthday. And suddenly I realized how petrified I was of parading in public. It was one thing being a weed in a garden of weeds, it was quite another popping my nettle head up in a bed of roses. I didn't fancy being stared at as a freak, even if I was one.

No, I couldn't possibly go. My mind was made up. Yet for some reason I was unable to bring myself to write back with a 'thanks but no'. And I found myself practising a study piece, a sonata for clarinet by Brahms, as well as two tunes from my sheet music, 'The Gypsy' and 'Paper Doll', over and over again until I got them more or less off pat.

The weeks passed and the fateful day was fast bearing down on me. I still hadn't written; I hadn't even asked what 'RSVP' meant in the bottom corner of the invitation card. Ted and Hilary were constantly urging me to go.

'Look, silly,' said Hilary, 'you've got to show your face sometime. What better way than for people to accept you on your own terms, through your music? You don't know how lucky you are.'

Ted's advice was more personal.

'Bill, I've never had a chance like this. If I had, I might not be here now. You'll be among music-lovers who'll judge you on your playing, not your looks. Not all musicians were oil paintings, you know. Take Liszt, he was an ugly old so-and-so with a big conk, yet he had all the society ladies swooning over him.'

I wasn't entirely convinced. But on the big day I put on my grey flannel trousers, clean shirt and tie, and a blazer lent me by another boy, Eric, who was about my size. And I stood outside the wrought-iron gates leading to the long drive, holding the invitation card in one hand and my clarinet and music in the other.

PRESENTS

At 12.45 sharp a silver grey Rolls Royce drew up
outside the gates, and a man in a peaked cap and
uniform got out, asking respectfully, 'Pardon me, sir, are
you William Riley?'

I nodded uncertainly.

With that he opened the rear door and motioned me
inside. And off we went.

11
The Maisky Visit

If the chauffeur had noticed my ugly mug, he was too well trained to show it; he kept his feelings to himself. Not that he took a close look at me; he sort of gave me sidelong glances, keeping his gaze respectfully lowered, like some lackey kowtowing to a Chinese emperor. He needn't have worried, I wasn't going to have his head chopped off for gazing on my sunny countenance. Once inside the car, he spoke only when spoken to, which was a relief; it gave me a chance to get my bearings and take in the countryside, then the suburbs, the town centre and urban sprawl, shading off into well-heeled districts with palatial houses screened from idle gaze by horse chestnut and weeping willow.

I did venture some questions, just to prepare myself.
'Who is Mr Maisky?'
'Will many people be there?'
'Is he a musician?'
To all three his replies were brisk and tidy.
'Mr Maisky, sir? A diamond merchant. Russian. Stinking rich. Left Russia after the Revolution, went to China, made his dosh in Paris and retired here.'
'How many guests? Couldn't say. They've laid on quite a do.'
'Musician? No. Music lover, yes; he lives and breathes it. Uses his money to support musical causes, including helping up-and-coming youngsters.'
For the rest of the journey I lounged back in the sumptuous leather seat, feeling like the Sheikh of Araby surveying the less fortunate as we glided past their Austin Sevens and Morris Minors. I couldn't relax completely, for each time I thought of the ordeal ahead

the butterflies in my stomach began to flutter wings as wide as a condor span.

I was concerned more about my solo debut than my appearance. After all, with any luck I'd be on a stage, at a respectable distance from decent folk. In any case, after all the skin grafts my parts were roughly back in place—eyes, nose, lips, ears, chin—even if they were like a patchwork quilt, especially when I got excited: some bits went red, some white, others stayed a codfish grey, rather like the underside of a copper frying pan.

Oh well, they'll have to take me as they find me . . .

I didn't really believe that. It was a phrase my mum would use when she hadn't time to put her make-up on.

All at once, my thoughts were interrupted by the limousine swinging into a driveway; it crunched over a gravel path leading to a garage as big as the terrace of two-up, two-down where I was born.

This Gulliver garage stood alongside the Maisky residence which is like saying a destroyer stood beside a battleship. The house reminded me of an old tithe barn I'd seen near Titchfield Abbey. It was a rambling old russet-yellow brick building with crooked windows, black timbers embedded in roughly whitewashed stone strips, gnarled creepers twisting up to the rose-slate roof, and a massive oak door set back in a glass-covered green porch.

It was certainly no concert hall. And with the nip and damp of early March in the air, I guessed they weren't planning to put on an open-air concert in the back garden. Surely I wouldn't be exposed to view in the centre of a drawing room, hemmed in by onlookers breathing down my neck. I'd seen pictures of such recitals in my Mozart book.

The chauffeur drew up outside the cavernous garage and advanced to open my door.

'Here we are, sir, all safe and sound, I trust.'

'Oh . . . er . . . yes,' I said, still confused. 'Ta very much.'

I was tightly clutching my clarinet like some lucky charm; I had a pressing need to keep close contact with the only familiar object I had with me. To tell the truth, I felt like a ship torn from its moorings on a dark stormy night. No Ted, no Hilary, no door to my room to shut on the inside, no quiet woods to wander through, no place to hide. I was panic-stricken.

The chauffeur noticed me shivering and must have thought I was going down with flu.

'Would sir follow me, please?' he said in alarm. 'Mrs M. will give you a mug of hot cocoa to put some colour into those cheeks.'

I gladly fell in behind him as he marched smartly down the side of the house, peaked cap under one arm. He evidently wore his natty dove-grey cap only inside the car and took it off outside. An odd custom, especially as a spattering of rain was wetting my own unprotected head.

He rapped his knuckles sharply on the glass panel of the door and took a step backwards, head slightly bowed. When a maid in black dress and white cap and apron opened the door, his serious look mellowed to a smile.

'Oh, hello, Betty,' he said cheerily. 'One young musician for the delivery of.'

Betty's half-smile turned quickly sour as she caught a glimpse of the little monster in black blazer and grey trousers standing behind the chauffeur.

'Oh lor'!' was all she could manage.

Then, swiftly recovering herself, her expression of horror twisted to one of pity. Unlike the chauffeur, she obviously had not been primed to expect Frankenstein's brainchild. A further confusion was that she knew *her* place, but what was *mine*?

Was a musician an honoured guest, a celebrity, or just

another menial? As if interpreting her thoughts, the grey-uniformed man spoke sharply to her, 'Come, come, Betty, don't keep the young *sir* waiting; he'll catch his death of cold out here in the drizzle. Take him to Mrs M. at once.'

His accent on the '*sir*' told her all she needed to know about my station and she quickly pulled herself together.

'Sorry, Albert, sorry, sir,' she mumbled, red in face and neck and averting her gaze. 'Yes, do come in, young sir. Please wipe your feet and wait here in the hallway. I'll inform Madam immediately.'

I stumbled over the step, dutifully wiped my shoes on the coconut mat, and ran five fingers through my wet hair, slicking down the wayward tufts. I stood there awkwardly for a few minutes, hands behind my back, clarinet and sheet music under one arm. Soon I heard a booming bass voice with a strong foreign accent.

'Breeng heem een, *bednyashka*, breeng heem een!'

Advancing towards me down the long hallway, arms outstretched, was the most formidable woman I had ever seen. To say she was big was like calling a battleship a boat. She was built like a barn door, solid rather than fat, lofty rather than tall, an all-in wrestler of a woman who looked as if she could uproot trees with one hand.

She was upon me before I could move, embracing me in a bear-hug, so that my face got squeezed into the bulging bolster of her bosom.

'Oi-yoi-yoi, *Gospodi*, *bedny malchik*! Beelee, Beelee, welcome, little pigeon.'

Whatever that meant, I took it as a kindly welcome; I guessed the 'Beelee' was me. When I came up for air, my first thought was for my precious clarinet. Had she ground it to sawdust?

Luckily, it still seemed to be in one piece, though the reed and mouthpiece were skew-whiff; I twisted them back into place as she stared at me with not a flicker of revulsion on her beaming face.

'Forgive me, I so pleased to see you,' she boomed.
'You Eengleesh so skeenee. I hear you play Mozart—ees
vonderful, *choodno*.'

Only then did she notice my wet hair and blazer; at
once she turned to Betty and gave instructions for me to
be dried off and warmed up.

As Madam turned on her heel, Betty took my arm and
led me into the kitchen where she sat me down and
handed me a clean white towel. I hadn't yet had a
chance to say a word—perhaps they thought I was deaf
and dumb as well as ugly?

I was so busy drying my hair that I didn't hear
footsteps approaching the kitchen. When I caught the
sound of a chair scraping behind me, I turned to see a
small, bald-headed man wearing old fashioned pince-
nez. He was shyly staring at the rough surface of the
wooden table as if he were the butler or footman. When
the man spoke I realized with alarm that this must be
Mr Maisky.

'T'anks for coming, Villiam,' he said. 'Vat vill you
play?'

I jumped up to face my host, sticking out my hand
awkwardly. Unlike his wife, Mr Maisky winced as he
caught full sight of my face. At once he noticed the pain
in my reaction.

'I know my eyes betray vot my mind sees,' he said
frankly. 'I hate myself for it, but I can't help it. I beg
forgiveness.'

How very un-English! I thought.

'That's all right, sir,' I said, trying to put him at ease.
'Everyone does it. I'm used to it.'

He frowned, still cross with himself.

'I thought I'd play a couple of songs,' I said, '"Paper
Doll" and "The Gypsy", followed by the Brahms
Sonata for Clarinet, if that's OK.'

A brief smile flitted across his face as he said quietly,
'Ah, I'm pleased you found my gift useful.'

Oh, right. So this was the source of my Christmas present. My look of surprised recognition obviously embarrassed him for he threw up his hands.

'Brahms loved gypsies, and probably paper dolls as well,' he said with a laugh. 'Come, my boy, let me show you vere you and my other musician friends vill perform. No doubt you vant to get feel; we've a good hour before start.'

He led the way down the long hallway and out through the back of the house; we walked down a wet path across the garden, past some willow trees . . . and there before me was the site of my first solo concert performance. A cowshed!

12
Cowshed Serenade

Mr Maisky giggled into his hand at my disappointment.

'Cows luff moosik!' he said between fits of giggles. 'But don't vorry, we haff no moos or poos to disturb you. Come.'

He led the way through thick wooden doors into the cowshed. Appearances certainly can be deceptive! Once inside the high-beamed wooden shed, I began to appreciate Mr Maisky's genius for turning water into wine, glass into diamonds, cowsheds into concert halls.

I saw no cow stalls, no mucky straw, no mangers or cobblestone gullies to empty out the cow streams. Instead, there was a simple plank floor, rows of church pews, unpainted timber walls and, at the far end, a sturdy stage bearing a grand piano and five or six music stands; in the wings dark red plush curtains hung down from a brass rail.

'Wow!' I exclaimed, my eyes shining with admiration.

'*Kontsertny zal imeni S. V. Rachmaninova*,' he said with a flourish, translating for me, 'The Rachmaninov Concert Hall. All in my own backyard!'

He beamed all over his round face, visibly proud of being able to indulge his favourite hobby. He clearly loved music with a passion.

'Now, Beelee,' he said, rubbing his hands, 'I'll let you get feel of ze place. I hope acoustics suit you.'

And off he trotted through the rain, humming to himself.

I advanced down the aisle, lost in this topsy-turvy world, past the church pews towards the steps leading up to the stage. One consolation was that I'd be at a fair distance from all but the long sighted; hopefully, they'd focus more on the music than the player.

As I slowly climbed the six steps I wondered at the clip-clopping echoes of my footsteps reverberating round the walls, up to the vaulted roof, bouncing off the old timbers and rolling down the chamber. Old man Maisky needn't fret: the acoustics would suit my style a treat.

Unwrapping my instrument from the old towel I kept it in, I examined the damage that the female Grizzly Bear had caused. Nothing serious, apart from a chipped reed. Luckily, I had a spare preserved in an old hanky. Once I'd changed the reed I put the clarinet to my lips and honked.

'Burrrpppp!'

I almost jumped out of my skin! What a racket!

The loud noise told me two things. First, I'd have to play more pianissimo than I normally did amidst the trees; second, I couldn't afford to fluff a single note—or it would stick out like a sore thumb.

Very cautiously and slowly I tiptoed up and down the scales in two separate keys, major and minor. Then I practised a few low notes followed by some squeaky high ones. Content with the basics, I launched into my repertoire.

Was this me? All by myself? It sounded so full and round as if an entire orchestra was filling the hall with sound. But if my playing pleasantly surprised me, so my occasional burp and squawk warned me of the pitfalls of complacency.

So engrossed was I in the sounds I was making that I didn't notice the time passing. I got quite a shock when the doors opened and a handful of raincoated men headed by Mr Maisky came in. Advancing towards the stage, the host announced, 'Villiam, I vant you meet your fellow musicians.'

Only then did I notice that they were carrying cases of

different shapes and sizes. One by one they clattered up the steps to shake my hand and introduce themselves.

'Roderick.' 'Geoffrey.' 'Boris.' 'Peter.' 'Godfrey.'

'Billy Riley, pleased to meet you,' I replied awkwardly.

All were grown men, two quite elderly. I won't say none of them seemed to notice my appearance, but it wasn't a big deal. We were all in this together, and I wasn't the only one looking white about the gills.

As the musicians unpacked their instruments, Mr Maisky took my arm and led me into the wings, round the back partition and into a narrow area filled with half a dozen wooden chairs and stools. Through the partition I could hear them warming up, the 'ding, ding, ding' of a piano note, the scrape of violins, rather more tuneful than Ted's, and the sound of two other instruments—I guessed a cello and a double bass.

'Now, ees der anysing you need?' asked my host.

'No, no, nothing,' I said. Then I added, half to myself, 'I'm a bag of nerves.'

'All musicians haff nerves,' he said with a smile. 'Let me give you tip. Before start, seek out sympasetic face in audience and play for zat person alone. And take time, Beelee, never rush music; listen to yourself play and enjoy sounds.'

I thanked him and said I'd try to follow his advice. He was clearly eager to get away:

'Now, relax while I go greet guests.'

As Mr Maisky disappeared, my 'colleagues' trooped backstage. All were wearing black dress suits, with a shiny stripe down the side of their trousers, white ruff shirts and black bow ties. And here was me in faded blazer, unpressed grey flannel trousers, grey shirt and tie I'd borrowed from Ted. 'Midnight blue', was how he'd described the colour. More like 'electrifying blue' I'd say.

They did their best to put me at ease, joking about the out-of-tune piano and poking fun at our audience.

'All buck teeth and toffee noses,' said Roderick. 'They couldn't tell a C minor from a Morris Minor.'

The minutes ticked by and I was surprised to see Godfrey the pianist take out a spotlessly white handkerchief and wipe his hands and brow; from his hip pocket he fetched a flask and took a quick swig.

'Ah, that's better,' he sighed. 'You know, William, I get butterflies every time I play. Never fear a few nerves.'

As he was speaking we could hear a cacophony of voices, coughs, high-pitched laughs, and the scraping of benches behind the partition. Then, all at once, a deep voice cut through the din and commanded immediate silence. It was the formidable Mrs Maisky.

'Ladees and Genteelmen,' she sang out. 'Our kontsert commences with Beethoven. Moonlight Sonata.'

Staccato applause was Godfrey's cue to wipe his hands once more, shake hands with each of us and step round the backdrop on to the stage. I whispered 'Good luck, Godfrey,' as he took my hand limply in his.

He need not have worried. It sounded absolutely perfect to me and earned appreciative applause. The recital continued with a duet, followed by a quartet and two solo numbers. I was relieved to hear Godfrey play 'Tea for Two' and 'Jamaican Rumba'; my two little melodies would not be so out of place, after all.

This was it: Mrs M.'s dulcet tones, 'Master Villiam Raileee, clarinet.'

Those who are about to die salute you . . .

13
My Debut

I stood up stiffly, as did all five of my colleagues; they waited in a row, as if a royal personage was about to shake their hands. Evidently, the handshake was a musical ritual—soft and limp so as not to damage wrist or finger. Their warm hands injected trust and confidence into mine before I marched boldly on to the stage.

To my surprise I was applauded even before I had played a note. It was good to know my fame had spread so far . . .

With a brief bow, I took up position in the centre of the stage; to my dismay, I felt and heard a creaking floorboard under my left foot. Rather than put me off, it took some of the solemnity out of the ordeal and gave me the giggles. Desperately I scanned the upturned heads for a friendly face. There she was. I picked out a kindly grey-haired woman who reminded me of Gran; her shining eyes seemed to be willing me to forget my nerves and play well.

In a rather shaky, squeaky voice I announced my two pieces.

'The Gypsy', 'Paper Doll'.

Then focusing on Madam Kindly Smile, I began to play. Slowly, confidently, squeezing every mellow note out of Terry Clough's gift.

At the end of the first tune, I lowered the clarinet with some relief, awaiting applause. Not a sausage. Whatever was wrong? Oh well, perhaps they were saving their hands for a double round after the next piece? Quickly I went into 'Paper Doll', determined to make it swing down the hall and round the walls.

It sounded fine to me and at the end my chosen lady gave me a smile of satisfaction, following the rest of the music lovers in a polite round of applause.

I bowed again and couldn't help myself: musicians, I know, are supposed to keep a straight face at all times. But I just stood there, alone on stage, grinning like a Cheshire Cat. Then, gathering up my music, I took my grin into the wings, expecting a dressing down from my new-found friends. Instead, they seemed genuinely pleased.

'Well done, sonny,' said Roderick. 'That's half the job done. Mind you, the second half's usually a doddle after the audience's soaked up the champers.'

In next to no time the coughs and sneezes returned to their seats, and the sergeant majorette's voice boomed out again. For the second half of the programme, I was due on next to last, after the Borodin and Tchaikovsky string quartets. To tell the truth, I was so carried away listening to the beautiful music that I didn't even hear myself announced. It was only when Boris the cellist gave me a nudge that I came to my senses.

'You're on, William. Give it to 'em, lad,' he whispered.

I was still partly in a trance when I walked on stage. How on earth could I follow the lovely melodies of the quartet? It was like the proverbial dustcart after the Lord Mayor's show.

But I sought out my lady fair and did my best. In fact, I had never put so much feeling into my playing and concentrated so hard. Was this really me? I followed Mr Maisky's advice and, for the first time, actually listened to myself. Whoever it was playing Brahms received a very long round of applause; and I was surprised to see the lady I had serenaded wipe away a tear with a mauve handkerchief.

I bowed low and this time kept a straight face as I marched smartly off into the wings where Godfrey was waiting.

'How the hell am I going to follow that?' he said miserably.

I knew it wasn't that good; but it was a kind gesture from one musician to another—or so I kidded myself. This time I gladly sipped a glass of shandy poured for me by the others.

As they resumed their hushed chatter, I reflected on my performance as critically as I could. I knew there was room for improvement. And now that I had got a taste for making music, I was hungry for more. Much more. But to improve I needed help, someone to take me further. How? Teachers cost money. They weren't for the likes of me.

Then, all of a sudden, another thought burst into my brain; and it stunned me. I had appeared in public, all by myself, in front of scores of 'outsiders'; I had shared jokes with fellow musicians . . . and I hadn't once given a thought to my appearance. Nor, I think, had they!

14
Daffodils

I walked back to the limousine standing outside in the rain, having survived another suffocating embrace from Madam Maisky. One hand was in my blazer pocket, feeling the white envelope her husband had slipped into my hand. 'For you, maestro,' he had said.

When I was safely on the home run, I could contain my curiosity no longer. Taking the long slim envelope out of my pocket, I slipped a thumbnail under one end of the flap and carefully slit it open, taking care to tear only along the gummed flap.

Inside were two notes.

One was a stiff oblong visiting card with an address in one corner and a big handwritten message in the middle:

WITH APPRECIATION
Alexander Maisky

The other was a folded white sheet of paper.

Flattening it out, I was surprised to see the king's head and the caption 'Pay the bearer on demand the sum of five pounds'. I assumed this must be a five pound note, though I'd never seen one before. My long whistle of astonishment startled the chauffeur.

'Is everything all right, Master William?' he asked.

'I don't really know,' I said. 'Can you tell me: is this five pounds?'

He squinted in his mirror, pursed his lips, then made up his mind, 'It certainly looks like it.'

I was still dreaming of all the things my five pounds could buy when I noticed us driving through a pretty village close to Boniface. Suddenly I had an idea. I'd seen a notice 'Flowers for Sale' outside a thatched house on our trip to town. Now, on an impulse, I asked Albert to stop.

Too embarrassed to buy flowers myself, I said, 'May I ask a favour, please? Would you go and buy a nice bunch of flowers—they're for a friend.'

'Certainly, sir,' he said with an understanding smile.

He pulled over in front of the thatched cottage, got out of the car and came round to me; I handed over my crisp five pound note and off he went down the winding path, holding my money in a gloved hand as if it were the crown jewels.

When he returned, he was carrying a big bouquet of daffodils, which he laid on the seat beside me before counting out the change.

'You'll have to get yourself a purse, sir, if you stay in the music business,' he said. 'Or open a bank account.'

I had no idea what a bank account was, but he was right: for the first time in my life I did need a purse.

In less than ten minutes we were cruising down the driveway to Boniface Home. Albert shook my hand in farewell, though I could only offer three fingers with my arms full of flowers, sheet music, and clarinet.

'It's been an honour, young sir,' he said. 'I do hope we meet again in the not-so-distant future.'

'Thanks very much,' I replied warmly.

I noticed that he had not removed his glove when shaking hands; that was probably to show he knew his place in the presence of such a celebrity as me!

As the silver Rolls circled our stone fountain and vanished through the shrubs and trees of the driveway, I pushed open the door with my shoulder and went in. Home Sweet Home! It was early evening: too late for tea and too early for our cocoa and biscuit supper.

I made my way slowly down the old familiar passageway and smiled as I caught the sound of music coming from my neighbour's room. I knocked on her door.

'Come in, Billy,' sang out Hilary.

'How do you know it's me?' I said through the door. 'It could be Vera Lynn or Winston Churchill.'

'I've been expecting you,' was all she said.

The door opened and a great bunch of daffodils floated in, filling the narrow room with the beautiful fresh fragrance of spring. Following behind was a young man with a smug smile all over his ugly mug.

'This is for putting up with my racket,' I said.

'Oh, Billy,' was all she could utter as tears started in her eyes and rolled down her red cheeks.

To fill the awkward silence that followed, I answered her unasked question, 'Yes, well, it went OK, I suppose. I serenaded about sixty arty types in a cowshed, met a Russian who helps young hopefuls, and got smothered by a giantess who called me her "little pigeon". That's about it. Oh yes, and I was driven there and back by a chauffeur in a Rolls Royce. Just the usual routine . . . '

Her eyes shone with genuine happiness and pride.

'Now it's back to earth with a thud,' I said.

She forced a squidgy noise through her tears:

'How could you aff-ff-fford flowers?'

'Oh, didn't I tell you? I earned myself five quid. Money for old rope. More concerts like that and I might even consider buying this place. Anyway, I must write and tell Terry Clough my news. See you.'

I left her to arrange the flowers in jam jars, and entered my own room. Putting my precious clarinet on the bedside table, I gave it a gentle pat, saying, 'Thanks, my little Black Beauty. You and me could go places.'

Then I pulled out my exercise book from under a pile of library books, sat down on the bed and wrote a long letter to Terry, telling him all about the Aladdin's Cave his gift had opened up. So busy was I that I hardly noticed Hilary creep in to put a daffodil jar on my window sill.

DAFFODILS

That night I slept the sleep of the just. There was life out there after all, if only I could find some way to live it. I needed a magic wand to turn the gloomy daylight hours into rosy dreams of night-time.

Perhaps I already had a magic wand?

15
The Lucky Ides of March

It must have been a couple of weeks later, one showery afternoon at the end of March. My head was buried in Shakespeare's *Julius Caesar* at the time—I was preparing for my School Cert. exams—and I was mulling over the warning: 'Beware the Ides of March!' I had no idea what 'Ides' were, but I felt an awful dread that something was going to happen before the month was out.

It therefore came as no surprise, rather confirmation of my foreboding, when matron pushed open my door—she never knocked.

'Riley, you have visitors,' she announced. 'Two gentlemen. In my office *now*. Make yourself presentable.'

Could it be Brutus and Cassius come to do me in?

Sliding off the bed, I put on my Fair Isle pullover, slicked down my hair with water from the tap in my corner washbasin, and made my way down the dark corridor.

Matron's office was in the right-hand wing of our Home, just inside the entrance hall. I rarely passed through those dark portals that smelt strongly of Mansion polish and oak-wood panelling—matron gave us all the willies with her angry bark and withering stare. Behind her back we referred to her as Miss Gulch from *The Wizard of Oz*.

Now I had no choice. Thank goodness it wasn't a face-to-face encounter with the old witch. I could hear the two men's voices drifting down the hallway as I approached. I smoothed down my hair, pulled up my socks, and knocked on the door.

After a few moments, matron's loud voice penetrated the solid mahogany, 'Come!'

The two visitors had their backs to me, seated as they were in high-backed chairs before matron's massive oak desk. I stood, hands behind my back, just inside the door, awaiting further instructions. Evidently the conversation had been in progress for some time; I spotted two empty teacups and plates with cake crumbs on the little trolley separating the two men.

I could just make out a bald shiny head, a spiral of blue smoke, and a pair of highly-polished black shoes behind one chair. Above the back of the other chair rose a shock of unruly silver-black hair crowning a head that was hidden from me. It was the pepper-and-salt head that was doing the talking.

'Of course, he'd need to pass the entrance exams as well as audition; and he'd have to settle in, which won't be easy. It's a tough, dedicated, uncertain life. All that must be taken into consideration.'

His companion kept silent. Yet as he waved a hand to lift a cigar to the area of his mouth, I felt I'd seen that mannerism before somewhere, and recently.

I guessed the 'he' was me, though what the 'tough, dedicated, uncertain life' was remained a mystery.

'Sit down, boy,' said matron as if noticing me for the first time.

It didn't seem to matter to her that the only three seats in the room were taken. Perhaps I should sit on the floor . . . or on the edge of her desk?

'No chairs, matron,' I mumbled.

'Well, don't just stand there, fetch one then!' she shouted irritably.

I went out and dragged in a metal and green-cloth chair from the hallway, sitting on it just inside the door.

'Closer, boy,' she ordered, 'where we can see you.'

'Yes, matron,' I whined in a cringing puppy voice.

'Yes, Miss Gulch. No, Miss Gulch. Three bags full, Miss Gulch,' I muttered under my breath.

I dragged my chair over the carpet to one side of the room, so that I stood between matron and the visitors. As I sat down again, staring at my boots, I stole a glance at the two gentlemen. My delighted surprise at recognizing Mr Maisky must have showed because he gave me one of his crinkly smiles and a comforting, ''Ello, Villiam. Ve meet again already. Good to see you.'

The other man, the 'lion's mane', held out a stiff arm and said in a formal tone, 'How do you do? Clarence Price.'

I didn't wait to see his reaction to my cute looks; I was too scared of matron's disapproving glare. I kept my eyes firmly on my boots as I mumbled, 'How do you do, sir.'

'Listen, Riley,' broke in matron, determined to show who was boss on her terrain, 'these two gentlemen have spoken to me about your future. It's an opportunity for you to make something of yourself, despite your disability. We've come to an arrangement.'

She had a habit of reminding us inmates of our disfigurement, as if to emphasize our dependence on her. She it was who determined our destiny and always knew what was best. From what she'd said it seemed I had no say in the matter.

Well, whether it was fear of the Ides of March, or the cockiness my solo debut had given me, I don't know. But to matron's evident horror, I asked a question, 'What *is* this opportunity?'

I posed the question in such a way that it was clear I needed to think it over. I could hardly believe it was my voice querying matron's judgement.

Mr Price eagerly jumped in before matron could dash cold water on the question.

'Master Riley,' he said, 'I was at the recital the other Sunday and I enjoyed your performance. I think you show promise, though some rough edges need to be smoothed out. Through Mr Maisky's generosity, we'd like to offer you a chance to join my school of music. Of course, as I was just telling matron here, we enrol only students of the highest calibre; we won't be doing you any favours because of your circumstances. Is that understood?'

I was too dumbstruck to do anything but nod. Had I got it right? They were offering me a place in a school for young musicians—*if* I got through the exams. And that was A GREAT BIG 'IF'.

'Mr Maisky has such faith in you,' continued Mr Price, 'that he is offering to pay your fees. In fact, he will also provide private coaching for the practical exams.'

'I have to say,' interrupted matron, 'that William is one of our star pupils.'

Good for her, I thought. It's about time she stuck up for me. Or maybe she was keen to see the back of me.

'I dare say, good lady,' said Mr Price. 'But the entrance exams involve more than the three Rs: William must be able to read music well and play set pieces flawlessly.'

Matron had no ear for music, so that put a musical sock in her mouth. Mr Maisky came to our aid.

'Vell, a star pupil is a star pupil. If he has talent, he vill pick zings up kvikly.'

'We'll see,' said Mr Price cautiously. 'It won't be easy, but we are willing to give him a chance.'

What I didn't know at the time was that Messrs Price and Maisky had been at loggerheads over me ever since hearing my Brahms. The school principal had grave reservations about anyone as badly disfigured as me performing in public: my looks would distract the listener from my music.

Mr Maisky argued the opposite: my music would distract people from my appearance.

'Only if the music is exceptional,' Mr Price had maintained.

'But zat is your responsibility,' Mr Maisky had retorted. 'You must take the uncut glass from the rock and fashion it into a sparkling diamond.'

In the end, the Russian had his way, and the school principal had agreed to give me a chance. The rest was up to me.

So it was, once a week for six months, a tall, pale young woman named Kate Donnely came to the Home to give me lessons: notation, pitch, time signatures, rhythm, general musical and woodwind history.

We did our practice in the drawing room since that was the only place with a piano. It was horribly out of tune and had more dud and jangly notes than good ones. But old Maisky sent a blind piano tuner to patch it up and provide Kate Donnely with an accompaniment to my clarinet.

She took me through all the scales, the study works in my new Advanced Primer, and the three set examination pieces for clarinet and piano: two by Schumann and one by Weber.

Playing duets certainly forced me to retain an even pace throughout the music. At first it was hard to keep up with Kate's piano playing. But she was the most patient teacher in the world—and, at the same time, a hard task-mistress.

Whenever I grew tired and complained of a sore mouth and chest, she'd say sympathetically, 'Right, five-minute break, drink a glass of water and you'll be as right as rain.'

'K-K-K-Katy, wonderful Katy . . . ' I used to sing under my breath when she'd gone, 'You're the only girl that I adore . . . ! Only I wish you'd go easy on me . . . '

Having a teacher made all the difference. I couldn't let her down: I therefore practised for a couple of hours twice a day, so as to be ready for the next session. It was what old 'Whitewash' called 'setting targets, one at a time'.

And although it was often boring, repeating the same old tune or scale over and over, I got such a kick out of seeing Kate's smile of pleasure that it made it all worthwhile.

Whether I'd be up to audition standard was another matter . . .

16
Whitewash's Warning

The audition was two days short of my seventeenth birthday, on 8th October. But before auditioning I had a hospital date for tests; ominously, my next of kin—Gran—had been asked to accompany me.

Would old 'Whitewash' throw a spanner in the works? I hadn't thought to ask whether my damaged lungs were up to a whole lot of blowing. Who knows, my musical career could go up in smoke, like my lungs, before it had begun. I tried not to think of it. The last time my features had come under the microscope was six months ago, just before Kate had appeared on the scene. And I got a clean bill of health.

I'd never felt better. True, my pair of scorched bellows were tone deaf and hated music. They wheezed and whined whenever I hit the high notes or did my fortissimo. By now I'd come to accept a bit of pain as part of the price to pay for making music. But what long-term harm was I doing?

'Whitewash' was about to tell me.

Gran was late. Or, rather, her bus, train, bus, taxi rides did not overlap, and she'd had several frustrating waits. But she was as perky as ever, concerned only for my well-being, and for the 'poor little darlings', as she called my fellow sufferers. And she had brought a little something for Harry, our van driver, who was champing at the bit.

'For your chest,' she said. 'A wee drop of the Irish.'

It seemed to do the trick, for Harry forgot all the injuries he had threatened to inflict on my family for making him wait nearly an hour.

Off we drove, the three of us, for our rendezvous at

the old familiar burns unit. It was one of those sunny autumn days which for some reason people called an Indian summer—though I'd have thought summers in India were stifling.

Sun or no sun, I was far from feeling summery: I had the shivers and shakes, the foretaste of a bad cold; I was sneezing all the way to the hospital. The night before matron had insisted on putting mustard plasters on my chest and rubbing hot camphorated oil on my neck. Neither helped, though I smelt exotically of mothballs soaked in mustard and cress.

My big worry was of being sick for my audition.

Unusually I wasn't directed to the surgery for examination. Instead, a nurse escorted Gran and me to Mr Whiteway's office. Unlike the pea-green spartan clinic, it was a cosy room with a coal fire burning in the grate, and two fawn armchairs and a settee standing on a Persian rug. A small desk and chair were tucked away in the corner. The air smelt oddly of mint humbugs.

'Whitewash' was his usual self: deadpan face and evidently wishing he was somewhere else. To put us and himself at ease, he began by asking Gran about her health. That was a mistake. After five minutes of her list of ailments, he had to interrupt her and turn to me.

'Nothing serious then, Mrs Murphy. Now then, William, this isn't a prod and poke day. But I do need to test your lungs; take off your jacket and sit over here.'

He indicated the chair by his desk. When I was sitting down, my jacket in Gran's hands, he lifted my shirt and applied his cold stethoscope first to my back, then to my front. Saying nothing except the occasional 'mmmm', 'aahhh', and 'uhnnn', he then put an orange rubber tube in my hands and commanded, 'Blow into the tube as hard as you can.'

The tube was attached to what looked like a metal jug of water; and as I blew down one end, the water rose up the narrow glass window at the side.

WHITEWASH'S WARNING

'Harder!' came the command.

I did my best until my lungs felt fit to burst. A sharp pain shot through me, as if a dagger had been thrust in my chest.

Still saying nothing, the surgeon noted the height of the water mark on the jug and wrote down some figures on a notepad. Gran and I sat patiently, keeping a reverent silence, awaiting the verdict on my blowing test. Would I be allowed to play blow-football again or to blow bubbles through a straw?

He looked up from his note-taking and stared at me as if I were a condemned man; he then heaved a sigh that seemed to travel up from his shiny brown brogues. This was it: how much longer did I have to live?

'William.'

We waited as he sucked on his pen top.

'We've come a long way, you and I,' he said at last. 'I've done all I can for you. I can do nothing more. I'm due for retirement at the end of the year, so this'll be our final consultation. I wanted your gran to be present because what I have to say concerns your entire future.'

He paused and looked steadily at Gran whose eyes were fixed on the meaty hands folded in her lap.

'That old bomb turned a silk purse into a sow's ear, so to speak. And we've done our best to switch the clock back. To some extent we've succeeded: the skin grafts have taken well and you are reasonably presentable. But you know the limits of what can be achieved. From now on, all we can do is let nature take its course.'

He sighed again, keeping the worst news back in order to soften the blow. Now he came straight out with it.

'That fire did permanent damage to your lungs. Nothing can be done; you'll just have to live with it, I'm afraid.'

I couldn't hold back any longer.

'What about my music?'

He shook his head.

'Matron and I have had words over the phone,' he continued in a strained voice. 'I know all about your progress and the music school opportunity. So I realize how big a blow this must be for you. Perhaps I should have warned you earlier. Any sustained pressure on your respiratory system could result in a collapsed lung. That's too big a risk to take.'

I felt as if my whole world as well as a lung was collapsing. Gran had taken my hands in hers and was squeezing sympathy into them. I couldn't believe it. I wouldn't accept it. I began desperately clutching at straws.

'But I have two lungs: if one goes pop I can still use the other.'

'True,' he said, stroking his chin. 'One of your lungs is fairly strong. But it's a big risk.'

His admission opened up a window of hope; and it reinforced my determination to fight. I wouldn't give up now. Not after regaining my confidence, finding a reason for living. I looked Mr Whiteway straight in the eye.

'I remember you telling me to have faith in myself,' I said. 'You gave me the will to fight. You said, the only way to be accepted back into society was to get out there and live life to the full. I promised you I'd try.'

Now it was his turn to look down at his hands.

Mine were the last words.

'I'm going to do just that.'

17
Teddy Bears' Picnic

I said nothing to my music teacher about the fateful hospital visit. She had driven up early on the morning of the audition to take me to the music school; it was a long haul, about an hour's drive, and we wanted to get there in good time.

I'd never taken a proper music exam before or had an audition. But Kate had prepared me as best she could, going through test papers and numerous repetitions of the set pieces. I practised until the music was coming out of my ears; I even continued to finger and blow in my sleep.

We set off bright and early in Kate's red MG sports car. She had lent me an old black case for my clarinet, so I now carried it by the handle like a plumber with his bag of tools. Besides my instrument the case contained a clutch of secret weapons to ensure success: a pressed four-leaf clover wrapped in a starchy white hanky, from Hilary; a good luck card with a black cat on, from the Clough family; an old chicken wishbone bound with a pink silk ribbon, from Gran; even a lucky stone with a hole in, from Sis.

With charms like that how could I possibly fail? They had already cured my cold.

Kate and I exchanged few words on the way.

'I like to concentrate on the road,' she'd said. 'And you need every spare moment for revision.'

Some hope of that. This was a rare outing and I wasn't going to miss it; it was also a chance to unclutter my mind before the ordeal. So I watched the world go by.

A mother was pushing a pram with one hand and

holding her child's hand with the other, no doubt on the way to school. The little boy was dragging his feet, obviously uncomfortable in his new school uniform: floppy grey cap, oversized grey blazer complete with red phoenix badge, short grey trousers, grey socks and black shoes—a child going to a fancy dress ball dressed as a mouse . . .

It reminded me of my own first day at school: Mum pulling her reluctant son to the local Infants, my heart-broken tears on parting, and my joy at being reunited with her at three o'clock. But the trust was broken, and I'd never believe her promises again.

There our paths diverged: this little lad would grow up in peacetime. No bombs, no sirens, no Messerschmitts. No scars, no pain, no hospitals. No one to lock him up in a home to shield him from stares and catcalls. No one to take his parents away: they'd always be there for comfort, for help, for love. They didn't have to lie to him . . .

Two lives: his and mine.

It wasn't fair.

I was putting myself in the wrong frame of mind for the coming audition, so I wrenched my thoughts away from personal woes, wound down my window a few inches and listened to the birds. By now our summer visitors—the swifts and swallows—had flown away to warmer climes.

But the songsters remained: the blackbird and thrush, as well as the less musical starling, sparrow, and finch. And as we drove through the countryside, their high-pitched soprano blended with the mellow baritone of the wood pigeon.

I imagined playing my clarinet in a bird orchestra, picking up their melodies, improvising, waiting for my solo spot against their background chorus. In future I would listen to nature more, try to write down music based on what I heard in the woods: the rustle of the leaves, the sighing of the wind, the patter of the rain, the song of the birds. I closed my eyes and played the set pieces through in my head—perfectly. I must have nodded off, for the next thing I knew the car had pulled up in front of a big stone house on a quiet country road.

The board beside the entrance said:

School of Music
(founded 1938)
Principal: Mr C. Price, B.Mus., M.Ed., FRCM
ARS GRATIA ARTIS

If the school was only ten years old, the country house, like Boniface, presumably once belonged to some bigwig family fallen on hard times. Still, it was being put to good use, and its one-time owners would surely have approved of young talent growing within their walls. My reverie was cut short by Kate's voice.

'Come, William, we've only got ten minutes.'

Pitched straight into battle . . .

I followed my chaperone through the entrance and into a marble hallway. A receptionist just inside the doors directed us to Room 24 at the end of the long corridor on the left.

I felt quite at home amidst the splendour of a country mansion, having spent the last four years in one. To the manner born! Here the main feature was a grand mahogany staircase cascading into the black and white marble squared hallway. I could picture ladies and gentlemen making their stately way down the stairs for a grand ball.

But apart from the internal decor and elegant past, there the similarity ended. For instead of creeping stick insects and praying mantises, this cathedral of the arts was full of worker ants and busy bees, purposefully going about their lives, not idling their time away. And they did so against the pleasing background of musical sounds: a trumpet climbing up the scales somewhere high above me, a violin pizzicatoing, a piano being sweetly caressed through a door to my right.

Music to my ears.

Not only that, the passers-by were more intent on the task at hand than on me. So although expecting the usual stares when exposed to public view, I found myself totally ignored, as if I was a fellow student with my own job to be getting on with.

Through a maze of corridors we finally arrived at a crowd of thirty or more young boys and girls, milling round a closed door. Some gave me a cursory glance as I approached, but none stared; most seemed too excitedly nervous to focus on anything other than THE EXAM.

At two minutes to eleven the doors swung open and a stern voice boomed, 'Sit down, settle down, do not commence until I say so!'

With a 'good luck' pat on the shoulder from Kate, I hurried to the back of the room and bagged a corner seat at a battered oak desk. Each desk top carried a face-down exam paper alongside a sheaf of lined paper. I glanced to my left where a sickly-looking youth in specs was fumbling in a pencil case. Seeing my look he must have thought I was making faces at him for he spilled his pencils all over the floor and almost burst into tears.

The stern voice belonged to a small round man in a dark suit who reminded me in shape and voice of Tubby the Tuba. The voice oompahed again, 'Print your names clearly at the top of the sheet. Then turn over the examination paper. You have precisely one and a half hours. You may begin.'

Silence. Or rather muted scratching, sniffing, ticking, and distant music.

The exam was in two parts: Musical Theory and Musical History; the latter itself was divided into two: General and Specialist. For Specialist we had to choose among Percussion, Strings, Brass, and Woodwind. My family was woodwind and my relatives were flute, piccolo, oboe, bassoon, and cor anglais.

Here goes. 'William Riley.'

Question One: 'Name the Musical Notes and Draw the Rest Values.'

Good. I had a reasonable memory, so I rattled off the notes with no trouble: 'Breve, semibreve, minim, crotchet, quaver, etc.'

The rest values were trickier and had to be drawn accurately on a stave printed on the exam paper.

All went passably well until I reached the General History section: I stumbled over members of the Bach and Strauss families and mixed Haydn up with Handel. Luckily there was only one W. A. Mozart and I got stuck into him with relish. The trouble was I was still writing about Mozart when Tubby the Tuba sang out, 'Ten minutes more.'

Help! I hadn't even started on the clarinet history questions. I scribbled down as much as I could before time was up.

'STOP WRITING NOW!'

'NOW' brooked no argument. I put down my pencil half-way through 'The first mention of the clarinet in any score is in 1720 in a mass by J. A. J. Faber . . . '

I had noticed that 'Specs' next door had finished writing some ten minutes earlier. He was now staring into space and blowing out his cheeks as if practising for his audition. He must be a trumpet or trombone, I decided.

As we made our way out, 'Specs' looked over his hornrims and hissed, 'I'm jolly glad that's over. It wasn't too bad, don't you think?'

He meant well, I suppose. But his 'It wasn't too bad' translated to me as 'dead easy', which it certainly wasn't in my book. My heart dropped into my boots as I tried to put on a crooked smile.

'I got a bit stuck for time,' I mumbled.

'Oh, really?' he said with a superior smile.

Never mind. At least he treated me more as a fellow hopeful than a sideshow freak. Or perhaps his eyesight was faulty.

It was a huge relief to find Kate waiting in the corridor.

'How did it go?' was her first question.

I shrugged.

'Come,' she said. 'We've over an hour before your audition. Why don't we go for a wander outside and find a dry spot for a picnic. I've a little hamper in the boot of my car.'

Dear, dear Kate. She knew I wasn't ready for display as a curio yet; that was the last thing I needed before my most important performance to date. So we walked through the trees at the back of the house, marking time to Kate's singing of 'The Teddy Bears' Picnic':

'If you go down to the woods today, you're in for a big surprise . . . '

I put the exam out of my mind and joined in the chorus:

'Picnic time for Teddy Bears . . . '

We both laughed at the tops of our voices as we sat down beneath a chestnut tree and sampled our banquet of lemonade, crisps, and bloater and tomato paste sandwiches.

18
Sour-Sweet Music

Kate had already scanned the audition lists and located W. Riley in Room 4 at 2.30. I was a bit burpy after the fizzy lemonade, so it was just as well I got all the gas out of my system beneath the chestnut tree. As Zero Hour approached, I began to feel a flutter in my guts and a jangle in my nerves.

By the time I set off for Room 4 I was shaking like a jelly on a plate. It didn't help bumping into 'Specs' as he came out of a nearby room carrying a violin case in his hand and a smarmy grin on his face.

'Piece of cake,' he said loudly for my benefit.

If he thought the remark would put me off, he was wrong: just the opposite. It made me mad. And anger overcame my nerves, replaced putty with steel. My grip on the clarinet case tightened as I knocked on the door of No. 4; and at the word 'Enter' I marched boldly in with Kate following on behind. My brash entrance was accompanied by a chirpy, 'Good afternoon, gentlemen.'

Two of the three examiners sitting behind their table nodded curtly; the third, a woman, made no response. Realizing my mistake, I quickly corrected myself, 'Sorry: lady and gentlemen.'

Ignoring my attempts to be chummy, the man in the middle said wearily, 'When you're ready, Riley—it is Riley, is it not?'

'Yes, sir,' I replied, deflated. I consoled myself that no one had so far shown a flicker of interest in my looks— or even in me as a person for that matter.

The desks had been shoved back to make space for a music stand; it was pitched a few feet from the table behind which the three solemn judges waited. Kate took her seat, sideways on to me, at a baby grand over by the window.

Unhurriedly, I placed my case on a desk, undid it and took out my music and clarinet. An hour before I had transferred the lucky charms to my pockets, so I was well equipped to put the mockers on them if they got stroppy. Fitting the study book into the stand, I blew the dust from my lungs down the clarinet tube and gave Kate a swift glance.

I could see that she was the nervier of the two, although she did her best to squeeze out a reassuring smile. I stood awaiting the first command.

Again the middle man spoke.

'Start with two scales: F Major and C Minor.'

Anything you say, boss. I can do them blindfold. 'Piece of cake,' as 'Specs' would say.

It doesn't pay to be too cocky. As I put the instrument to my lips and started to trip up the F Major stairs, I fluffed the third, fourth, and fifth notes, to the obvious irritation of old misery-guts.

What was I to do? I could see my Golden Opportunity rapidly slipping down the plug hole.

I stopped, removed the reed from my mouth, put one hand in my pocket and took out Hilary's starched handkerchief. Then, casually wiping my hands and mumbling an apology, I thrust the hanky back and returned the clarinet to my dry lips.

'Now, nice and steady does it,' I told myself.

And off I went again: F Major followed by C Minor. This time without a hitch. Thank God for that!

'Turn to page seventeen of your book,' came the next command, 'and play that study piece.'

Did I detect a softer note in his voice?

Quickly finding page seventeen, I ran through the study piece with barely a glance at the music.

'Thank you, Riley,' said the spokesman. Turning to

Kate, he asked, 'Are you ready, Miss Donnelly? The two Schumann and the Weber, if you please.'

I kept my eyes fixed on Kate's ponytail bobbing up and down as she ran through the introduction to my first set piece and, when she gave a deep nod, I came in on cue. Almost at once I cast everything out of mind: the judges, the classroom, 'Specs', the solemnity of the moment—and I soared away on swan's wings, transported to a magical land of musical dreams. For the next half hour I was in the safe keeping of my music: entranced, inspired, at one with Kate's piano.

Only as I went to lower my clarinet did I feel the searing pain in my chest; it immediately brought back vivid images of the bomb shelter. I did my best to conceal the agony inside me as I nodded gratefully to Kate and tried to read the three deadpan faces.

There was a long pause before anyone spoke. Then, evidently out of habit, the chief judge said briskly, 'Thank you. That will be all. You'll be informed in due course.'

Kate and I made our way out of the room. As soon as the door closed behind us, I pointed to my chest, unable to summon breath for speech, and I headed for the lavatory. It was a good ten minutes before I emerged, having doused the fire by sucking gallons of water from under the tap. Poor Kate looked pale.

'What on earth's the matter?' she asked.

'I'm OK now,' I wheezed. 'It's the price of fame!'

I attempted a laugh, but only set off a fit of coughing. Taking me by the arm, Kate hurried out into the fresh crisp air of mid-afternoon. We wandered arm-in-arm through the trees, not uttering a word. Purely by chance we found ourselves back at our Teddy Bears' picnic spot.

'If you go down to the woods today you're in for a big surprise,' sang Kate. 'But what *will* the surprise be?'

'It'd take thunder and lightning to impress those three barrels of lard,' I said glumly.

'William, you've never played better,' she said kindly. 'And if they weren't impressed they must be stone deaf.'

That lifted my spirits and I whispered hoarsely, 'Kate, whatever happens, I want you to know how grateful I am. It's been a tough six months, but it was worth every minute to be able to play such wonderful music with you.'

She smiled and we wandered slowly back to her car, each with our own thoughts.

On the return journey Kate put a question she'd never asked before.

'Do you often get chest pains when you're playing?'

She deserved to know the truth, so I told her the whole sorry story, starting with the bomb and ending with 'Whitewash's' warning.

Kate gave no advice, made no judgement. She just raised her head and voice, reciting clearly:

'How sour sweet music is
When time is broke and no proportion kept.
So is it in the music of men's lives.'

'Mozart?' I enquired.

'It might well be,' she said with a wistful smile. 'He died a sour death for such sweet music. No, it is our own musician of the soul, William Shakespeare, speaking through King Richard the Second.'

'We all have our cross to bear,' I said.

19
Farewell, Boniface!

After the initial gust of questions from the Boniface bonny faces, interest in my performance steadily dwindled. To my huge relief. It seemed I had become a gleam of hope for everyone, a shooting star blazing a trail through the night sky. Where I could go, others might follow.

Such was the weight of responsibility on my shoulders.

Sorry, folks, you're in for a big fat let-down. My comet had fizzled out.

For the time being, however, Ted wandered lonely as a cloud, fiddling away like mad among his onions and cabbages. Hilary's aunt had arranged singing lessons for her niece, so I now had competition for musical time. She didn't have a bad voice, but it was more of a watery grey than a fulsome red. Even matron was to be heard more frequently at the piano, playing and singing her Salvation Army hymns.

Given time, we might form a band, put on masks and become a troupe of strolling players.

The trouble was my time was running out.

My seventeenth birthday had come and gone and I had a couple of months' grace before finding a job and moving to a half-way home—part of my rehabilitation into the community. Most half-way homes were run-down terraced houses, with 'normal' neighbours on either side. About four or five 'misfits' lived together, cooking, cleaning, shopping, learning to cope 'on the outside'.

I dreaded the prospect. The alternative was even worse: parking my bones on Gran or Sis, who both agreed to have me. But I was determined to make my own way, however tough it might be.

I heard nothing more from the school of music: no phone calls, no telegrams, no letters, no welcoming committee come to shake my hand. For a week afterwards I would hover each morning behind the front door, waiting for the first delivery of letters to tumble on to the mat. Nothing. Nix. Zero.

I had given up hope when one midday, by second post, a fat envelope flopped through the letter box. Purely by chance I happened to be passing on my way to lunch; and I glanced curiously at the address: W. Riley.

Hey, that's me!

Snaffling the letter before anyone noticed, I ran helter-skelter to my room and banged the door shut. Then, with trembling fingers I opened up the buff envelope, tugging out the contents: three separate sets of paper—a school prospectus, a scale of fees, and a one-page letter.

Smoothing out the letter, I covered the top half with one hand and read it sentence by sentence from the bottom up. Even the last words 'Looking forward to welcoming you at the start of Spring term, Yours faithfully, Clarence Price' did not register fully until I had devoured every word. Then I re-checked the name to make sure it was me.

YES! I WAS IN! I'D DONE IT!

Grabbing my clarinet, I kissed and hugged it as if it was the cutest doll in all the world.

'You little beaut!' I gurgled, mooning over its sleek black body.

I felt like jumping over the moon, swimming the Channel, doing a loop the loop; I danced round the room, holding my arms out like an aeroplane.

Who should I tell first?

Hilary, of course. I'd write to Terry Clough, Gran,

Sis . . . Then there was Kate Donnely, Mr Maisky and his cuddly wife. Oh no, I didn't have enough envelopes and stamps! I had to inform Ted, matron, Harry, the whole wide world. Who else was there? Mr Whiteway . . .

Suddenly, as I recalled the surgeon's warning, I realized the full enormity of what I was doing.

Billy boy, you know the dangers, old son. Will you put your life at risk? You could be a painter—can't draw for toffees! A scaffolder—can't stand heights! A sailor— get seasick! A teacher—what, with my mug!

Music is all that's left. Oh, blow it. Blow it or bust! There was no contest. I would blow, even if I bust.

When everyone heard the news I was congratulated as if I'd won the world heavyweight boxing crown. And when I finally departed for the school of music early in the New Year, I had to promise to return to give recitals when I was famous: 'Free of charge,' I said generously.

They all came to see me off—all except Hilary who had gone to live with her rich aunt before Christmas, though she wrote regularly on scented notepaper.

Iris's husband Fred picked me up in his brand new Ford; Gran sat nervously in the back with Sis as I climbed in next to the driver. Farewell, Boniface; Hello, Sweet Music.

We chugged down the frosty driveway for the last time. I gave no backward nostalgic glance: the Home had helped tide me over the 'lost' years, yet I felt no warm attachment to it.

I was like other kids evacuated in the war or sent away to boarding school; however well-meaning their new guardians and friends, they can never replace the love and sense of belonging of home. Nor can they lessen the misery of being torn away from mother and family.

The journey passed in cosy chit-chat. Sis was going to have a baby—a girl would be Marilyn, a boy Joseph William, half after me. That was nice. Gran had decided to celebrate her seventieth birthday by visiting her Irish birthplace for the first time in fifty years—'To recharge the batteries for the next seventy years,' she said. Fred had just gained promotion, which meant moving 'up north' to a new branch of his bank in the midlands.

As for me, I had little to say about the future; it was to be a completely new and unknown chapter in my book of life.

20
Two Chinamen

As I crossed the threshold of my new home, I was met by an old boy of the school; he escorted me to my 'dorm' in a neighbouring building. To my dismay, I found I was sharing a room on the top floor with four others!

This was diving into the deep end all right. Sink or swim. I was horrified at the prospect. Would my room-mates ask for a move once they saw me? Would they screen me off? It wasn't fair on them to have to live with a monster . . .

Fortunately, no other occupants were around, though two bedspaces were obviously lived in. I picked a tidy bed and cupboard in one corner and put my clarinet and suitcase on the brown quilt before going down to say my goodbyes to Gran, Sis, and Fred.

I felt terribly homesick as I waved goodbye to the disappearing exhaust fumes—even though I had no home to feel sick for.

Making my way back into the main house, I latched on to my escort, a young man some years older than me. He was friendly and patient, helping to sort out my timetable, pointing out the refectory and other amenities, answering my questions.

'You have to be in by ten each night,' he explained, 'unless you've got a pass. No booze allowed—but there's a country pub in the village where you can have a beer. You'll need a bike to get there though. The nearest town has a cinema, dance hall, shops, and even a theatre where we sometimes give little concerts. But it's a good forty minutes on the bus. You get your letters from the pigeon holes.' He indicated a wooden stand with little compartments lettered alphabetically. Noticing a packet under 'R', he exclaimed, 'Good gracious, you've got one already, you lucky blighter.'

He waited while I tore it open to find a note of welcome from Mr Maisky and what he called my monthly allowance—the princely sum of five pounds.

'What about music practice?' I asked. 'Are times and rooms set aside?'

'My, you're keen,' he said with a smile. 'What are you?'

'Clarinet.'

'You're lucky. If you were piano or something biff-bash you'd have to book. But just grab any vacant room—up to ten at night when they come round to lock up.'

I would have asked more questions but for the arrival of another newcomer. He was dark-haired, sallow-skinned, and reminded me of a Japanese baddie I'd seen in comics. My first reaction was probably similar to his on seeing me: dislike.

'Are you Hai Ren?' asked my companion. 'I'm Ben, this is William.'

We all shook hands awkwardly.

'Come, I'll show you to your room; you're in with William here. We're expecting one more new boy—a violin.'

On the return trip to the dorm, I told Ben I preferred Bill or Billy to William; I didn't want to get stuck with a fancy name from the start.

Hai Ren took the bed just inside the door, beneath the room's only window.

'Right, I'll leave you two to get to know one another,' said Ben, 'while I go in search of our third fresher.'

Being alone meant someone had to speak.

'What are you?' I forced myself to ask.

He looked at me oddly, obviously not understanding the question.

TWO CHINAMEN

'I Chinese,' he finally said. 'From Hong Kong.'

That broke the ice. Oh, so he wasn't a 'baddie' after all. I seemed to recall that the Chinese had been on our side in the war. I laughed.

'No, no, I mean what instrument do you play?' I said clearly and slowly.

I saw no obvious instrument—unless he was hiding a tin whistle or piccolo in his bag.

'I pianoforte,' he said with a broad smile.

Certainly English wasn't his forte; nor was Chinese mine.

We chatted as we unpacked our bags. I was surprised to see that Hai Ren had even fewer possessions than me. Suddenly, he startled me with a question:

'What happen your face?'

How rude and un-English! I didn't know whether to ask him what had happened to his face to make it so ugly, or to tell him to mind his own business. But his look was so innocent that I couldn't help smiling to myself.

I told him the story.

He sighed deeply.

'My mother, father too burn in war,' he said. 'Church mission bring up me, pay for music.'

Just then the door opened and a familiar figure walked in: it was 'Specs'.

His words of greeting put the lid on our relations.

'Don't say I've got to live with two slitty-eyed Chinks!'

For a moment I didn't know what he meant. Then it dawned on me that my slits for eyes qualified me as a 'Chink' in his book. Charming. In my best Charlie Chan voice, I said, 'We slitty-eyed Chinks welcome honourable four-eyed guest.'

That took him aback. He was just about to pay me more compliments when he obviously thought better of it. Turning on Hai Ren, he snarled, 'Get your rubbish

111

off this bed. I can't sleep without a window. I'm taking this bed.'

If it had been me, I would have tossed his violin case out of the window. But my new friend had to fight his own battles.

Silently, he removed his belongings from the bed and cupboard and took the bedspace next to mine. That was a consolation to me: at least I wouldn't have the ignorant oaf next to me.

We left him to it and went in search of the first meal in our new home.

21
Life at Music School

Life at the school was, like music, 'sour-sweet', in Kate's words. On the sour side, the studies and practice were very hard work: I hadn't realized how much I had to learn. As well as a full music programme, we had our ordinary school studies, like every other student.

Then there was the sour atmosphere in our room. One of the old residents, a violinist, took 'Specs's' side. The other was a quiet, withdrawn fellow, a flautist, who kept himself to himself. So we formed opposing teams: two violins versus piano and clarinet with a flute for referee. It didn't come to blows, but that's because we never crossed the divide. The violins knew not to push me too far, and they got little response from the piano.

One result of their hostility was to forge a firm friendship between the two outcasts, Hai Ren and me. That was the sweet side of life. We often played duets together. He was brilliant: not only was he gifted at music and inspired me to practise far harder than ever before, he also taught me Chinese breathing exercises which eased the pain in my chest. In exchange, I gave him confidence to stand up to the bullies, helped him with his English and explained the strange customs of his new homeland.

I never forgot my old friends. I wrote regularly to everyone, now that I could afford envelopes and stamps. After a while Ted and matron fell silent. I didn't mind. They had stayed behind in my old world and probably didn't want even to think of life outside its walls. Hilary was studying for her 'A' levels in preparation for a medical degree. Terry Clough now had two children and was Secretary of the Yorkshire Miners' Union; besides that he was hoping to stand for Parliament at the next election—'That would give us a public voice,' he had said.

Iris and Fred took a keen interest in my progress and always found time to write. As for dear old Gran, she found her Irish roots so deep she settled down with a long-lost sister in a cottage above Bantry Bay. The only person to visit me was Kate Donnely; and each time she came we played duets together, mostly the hits of the day: 'In the Mood', 'Lazy River', 'Oh, Susannah', that sort of thing.

Mr Maisky not only sent me manna from Heaven, he used to get his chauffeur Albert to fetch me every so often. Betty would have piles of sandwiches ready for me; Mrs 'Bonecrusher' Maisky would hug and kiss me, and dear old Maisky would bore me to tears with stories of his encounters with Stravinsky, Prokofiev, and Rachmaninov.

Sometimes I'd be expected to play for a circle of friends; but usually I'd be invited round for Sunday tea and a chat about music. One day Mr Maisky asked me to bring along Hai Ren, and the two of us performed duets in the cowshed. Mr and Mrs Maisky spoke halting Chinese picked up from their time in Shanghai before the war. So we all got on like a house on fire, gabbling away in an exotic mixture of English, Russian, and Chinese.

If it hadn't been for my two hostile room-mates I might have forgotten all about my disfigurement. Most of the time music became my personality, and people accepted me as musician first and war-scarred orphan second.

But it wasn't just a few fellow students who made life difficult. Music school or not, a compulsory part of our curriculum was PT and games. I guess this fitted the private school ethos—to produce 'rounded personalities'. As old 'Hitler', our PT instructor, put it,

'You weedy types can't go blowing, banging, and scraping without strong lungs and muscles!'

So every boy and girl had to do a period of physical training each weekday, and games on Saturday mornings. The only way to get out of it was with an 'excused-games' chit. But for that you had to have a dicky heart or some such ailment.

No excuses, no sick notes for me. I wanted to be treated as 'normal'. Little did I know what I was letting myself in for. It wasn't just the effect of physical exertion on my dodgy chest and wasted muscles; there was a more personal reason for embarrassment.

We all had to wear regulation games kit: baggy navy-blue shorts and white vest. That exposed me to public view, scars and all—including to the girls in their sector of the gym or playing field.

By now I was a gangling seventeen year old, acutely conscious of my body as never before. And to parade my blotchy, scabby limbs and puny torso before the world, especially the female part of it, was a giant hurdle to overcome. Every stare at my personal freak show was like a dagger in my flesh.

I told myself: 'Chest out, chin in, stand straight and walk tall like Terry Clough, a veritable god of war! Think of your assets: clear blue eyes, hairy arms, a shock of wavy brown hair neatly parted on the right.'

Within a week I'd given in. I couldn't stand the pain or the shame. But my request to be excused got short shrift from 'Hitler'.

'Are you dying, lad, or just a cissy scared of physical jerks?' he bellowed for all to hear.

My protest that I had a weak chest didn't wash.

'Fresh air and exercise—that's what you need, son,' he said. 'We'll make a man of you yet!'

Back at the Home, our most strenuous activity had been table tennis. No one needed a note to avoid PT since we were all classified as walking wounded. Now, however, I was the odd one out, and 'Hitler' didn't like 'square pegs in round holes', as he put it. To him we were all poor excuses for human beings, to be drilled, disciplined, made fit, and turned off the parade ground like identical chocolate soldiers.

'Hitler' was ex-Colour-Sergeant Davies of the Royal Marines—a beefy, red-necked man with bristling ginger moustache and spiky hair to match. His frequently-mentioned claim to glory was as services middleweight boxing champion; squashed nose, cauliflower ears, and mantelpiece full of silver cups were proof of his endeavours in the ring.

My sickly frame was a challenge to him. At least he didn't sneer or write me off. Just the contrary, he watched eagle-eyed over my press-ups, running on the spot, horse vaults, wall bar pull-ups. And if he caught me slacking he'd yell, 'Come on, you long streak of misery, more effort!'

The one thing he never did was mention my disability. He seemed to regard me as he would a wounded soldier: I was to be toughened up through bullying to make me forget all self pity.

So I did my damnedest to knuckle under to escape attention. The only concession was rope climbing: one look at my disfigured hands and even C-S Davies winced. While others strained and struggled up the ropes, therefore, I was left to run rings round the gym.

My friend Hai Ren was not a sporty type either. He bumped into the vaulting horse, fell sideways in the forward roll, and couldn't get off the floor to climb the rope. He, too, became the object of 'Hitler' 's ire. Once the whole class had to do an extra dozen press-ups because poor Ren fell off the rope.

That didn't please 'Specs' and his bullyboy mates. When 'Hitler' had left and I was taking a cold shower, I suddenly heard jeers and cheers from the gym. At first I paid no attention, but when I couldn't find Hai Ren I began to worry. When I returned to the gym, my heart dropped to my plimsolls. He was sitting naked in a huddle at the foot of the dangling rope, shivering with shame and fear. Our dear school chums had 'debagged' him and stuck his vest and shorts on the beam above the rope. There was no way he could run the gauntlet naked between gym and dorm; nor could I bring help or clothes since someone had locked the gym door.

One of us would have to climb the rope. And since Ren was sitting on the floor paralysed with fear, that left me. Anger gave me strength. I would *not* let the bullies win.

Just to grasp the knotted rope with both hands was agony as the coarse fibres bit into my thin layer of palm skin. And when I took all the weight on my hands, I couldn't help myself—I let out a loud yelp of pain. Somehow I hauled up my feet and curled them round the bottom of the rope, taking some of the weight off my hands.

Then, inch by inch, I clambered up, trying to ignore the terrible pain in both hands—my precious, delicate clarinet hands. How I reached the top I'll never know. Once there I tossed down the clothing and began to shin back towards the floor. But my grip was too weak and I came slithering down, running my palms through the rough, burning rope.

I landed in a heap alongside Ren, my hands a bloody mess; no torture could have been more excruciating.

We managed to escape from the gym through an open lavatory window.

Sweet victory at bitter cost. For several weeks I could not touch the clarinet with my stitched and bandaged hands. Ren and I told no one of our ordeal. Certainly, 'Specs' and his mates never mentioned the episode, though their sheepish glances at my bandaged hands were revenge of a sort for us.

In the long run, I think old 'Hitler' was right. Fresh

air and exercise did help to build up my strength and bolster my confidence. Games also gave me an inner strength, a will to win combined with a powerful team spirit. As in an orchestra, my contribution was integral to the overall performance of the team.

To my surprise, there was even one sport I became quite good at: basketball. Of course, it helped being taller than most other students; but I was also fairly nippy across the boards and accurate with my basket shots. To protect my hands I wore skin-tight rubber gloves. In no time at all, I found myself first a regular member of the school team, then its captain. We didn't win many matches against local colleges and factory teams—musicians are stronger in the head than in the arm. But we had a lot of fun.

Once again, sport taught me a lesson for life: respect comes from what you achieve, not how you look. And when my last-second winning shot brought us victory against a rival music school, I was the hero of the hour.

As I went up to accept the cup in our packed gym, even old 'Hitler' had a dew drop in his eye. Afterwards he took me aside.

'There's a place for lads like you in the Marines,' he said. 'And we've the best band in the country.'

I swear he didn't even notice I was unfit for soldiering!

Not all my social life was a bed of roses. Far from it. With my Body Beautiful I was not exactly a hit with the girls, though those I got to know were chatty enough. Ren and I started going to the pub in the local village; often we'd make up a party from college and sit in the pub gardens over a glass of beer or lemonade.

For the first time I found myself having to make conversation with girls, even flirting with them! Not that it got me very far. But it was all part of the learning process, and I gradually came to realize that my looks weren't necessarily a barrier to forming a relationship. It wasn't only with fellow students either; after a beer or two, I even plucked up courage to 'chat up' local girls who didn't seem too bothered about my appearance.

That testing ground, however, had unforeseen pitfalls. One evening, some local lads, emboldened by the demon drink, took exception to my friendly relations with 'their' women. And they started making loud comments.

'I see Frankenstein's monster's escaped again! Ooooh-errr—he could be heading this way!'

'Watch out Dracula doesn't kiss your neck, girls!'

I did my best to ignore the taunts, and the girls were clearly ashamed of the oafish yokels. But a school friend, the normally aloof flautist from my room, amazed us all by saying, 'If you don't shut up, I'll put my fist in your gob!'

The local lads were so stunned they sloped off to a corner, muttering darkly about 'toffee-nosed thugs'.

Yet that wasn't the end of it. As we were leaving, the landlord accompanied us to the door—we thought to apologize for the insults. Instead he stood there, arms folded, shuffling his feet, searching for the right words.

'Look,' he mumbled, 'I don't know how to put this. Personally I've nothing against anyone who's mental; but it's bad for business, see. Your mate here is putting off my regulars. So if you don't mind not coming again . . . '

He quickly dived back inside before the flautist stuck one on him.

We were too taken aback to respond immediately. For a moment we wondered who he could be referring to—which of us was the loony? Then it dawned on us more or less together: it was me, the misfit, the odd bod, the one who stood out like a sore thumb. Physical meant mental.

Once again I reflected how hard it is for some people to accept anyone who's different—whether with one leg, one arm, one eye, three eyes, black skin, red, white, and blue skin. They're different—and unsettling.

I didn't go to the pub again. The experience jolted my confidence. That's how it always is: you gain on one front, move forward, then lose on another and fall back again. My friends did their best to invite me out and occasionally I went to the cinema—it felt safer in the dark.

Yet I always lived in dread of being banned from showing my ugly mug in public.

22
Graduation

So passed two and a half hectic years. They didn't so much pass as whizz by. I had learned a great deal in that time, especially about coming to terms with my disfigurement. On the academic side, I gained four 'A' levels—French, German, Latin, and Economics; and I was now preparing for the music certificate.

Besides written examinations, the pass-out involved a concert put on by all graduates. This annual do was a grand affair held in the theatre of the nearby town. To us aspiring 'virtuosi', it was important also because 'scouts' for several major orchestras attended—and I was half hoping for a place in one of them, even though they were as rare and precious as gold dust.

I sent out invitations to everyone I could think of, well aware that some, like Gran, were too far away to come. Gran had sent a card with a shamrock on it, wishing me the luck of the Irish and writing a simple PS: 'Play for your mother.' The invitation cards were standard with the school's name inscribed in gold letters at the top and an RSVP to the School Secretary at the bottom. I had no idea who, if any, of my invitees would turn up.

Hai Ren and I were to play with the orchestra in the first half of the concert; for our solos after the interval, we decided to dust off the Mozart Clarinet Concerto transcribed for piano accompaniment. Besides being a graduation exam, the concert was a sort of talent contest with prizes awarded by a celebrity panel for each major instrument and a special silver cup for 'Musician of the Year'.

Needless to say, Hai Ren and I practised hard. No pub

trips, card games, or cinema visits for us; no girlfriends to distract us; just practice, practice, practice until ten each night. We'd have invaded the early hours of the morning if the caretaker hadn't chucked us out. And our room-mates didn't take too kindly to being woken up by serious swots like us.

On the day of the concert the boys had to try on their hired dress suits, the girls their long black gowns—at least those who didn't have their own.

I'd never paraded in a dinner suit before, and when Ren and I saw each other in baggy black coat and trousers, white shirt, and black bow tie, we laughed ourselves silly. How much easier it is to play in jeans and open-neck shirt than in starched collar biting your neck and tight-fitting trousers.

I had only played soloist in an orchestra at rehearsals. It was such a wonderful feeling to be in a team of musicians, each person playing a set part in the performance. You just floated on a cushion of sound which nursed and coaxed you along until your turn came—then off you soared on your own, but always with someone there to catch you and lift you up again. Never had I felt so inspired. I guess it's like being a footballer in a great team, with everyone playing their part to achieve success. I don't know if Mozart played football, but in his concerto I was centre forward and knocked in all the goals.

At around five o'clock we all packed into the school bus, carrying our music cases and wearing dress suits and gowns. Some were nervously joking 'You look like a zebra crossing with ears.' 'Better than Mickey Mouse with glasses and moustache!' It was a sweltering June day and by the time we reached the theatre we must have smelt as well as looked like animals entering Noah's Ark.

Hai Ren and I stuck together like Siamese twins. He hadn't sent out invitation cards since he had no one to invite; but through me he'd got to know Kate Donnely and the Maiskys, so he would recognize some friendly faces in the audience. We had no way of telling who else would be present. Even when the curtain went up it was impossible to penetrate the blackness beyond the footlights. And the applause that greeted our orchestral introduction was just a solid wall of sound.

No Gran to shout out 'Lovely, Willy!'—I thanked my lucky stars for that.

So when Ren and I took a bow after our solos, we saw only our conductor standing before the dazzling lights that divided the stage from the noisy dark void. It had gone well. We knew the music by heart, having rehearsed it until the notes were coming out of our ears; it was a matter of producing the right mood and sound, interpreting Mozart and playing to our strengths. Fortunately, our styles and personalities blended perfectly and we inspired each other to rise to new heights.

At least that's what we thought; what others heard could well be different.

At the end of the concert we all waited backstage for the winners' names to be called. To my huge disappointment the clarinet prize went to another student. I was pleased for her since she had worked very hard and would often ask me for advice. In a way I was even more upset when Hai Ren failed to win the piano prize. Oh well, at least we could console each other in mutual disappointment: who wants an old tin cup anyway?

We wondered who would be Musician of the Year. 'Specs' had taken the violin prize and was clearly expecting to add to his silverware; he stood confidently in the wings waiting for his name to be called.

The jury's verdict was just being announced.

'Ladies and gentlemen, the jury has had a problem this year. We found it impossible to separate two outstanding performers; so we decided to nominate *two* Musicians of the Year—William Riley and Hai Ren.'

Our long faces changed to looks first of amazement, then of delight. Fellow students slapped us on the back and pushed us towards the stage. 'Specs' couldn't disguise his envy, muttering dark threats against the jury and all other ignoramuses . . .

Linking arms, Ren and I emerged into the limelight to receive the silver cup, each grasping a handle and posing for photographs. We were too stunned to do anything but bow repeatedly and shake hands with the conductor. The audience seemed to go wild, clapping and shouting 'Bravo!' for several minutes. The only voice I recognized was Mrs Maisky's fog-horn: 'Vell done, Beelee. Vell done, Ren!'

When we finally escaped backstage, there was more congratulation from students and teachers before we all moved off to the reception. At last I was to discover if any of my invitees had witnessed my triumph.

23
Congratulations

In the crush of the reception it was hard to tell performers from concert-goers. Not that Ren and I were hard to spot. Also, since I was a tall gawky youth, I had the lighthouse advantage—easily seen and easily seeing.

The first homely face I recognized was Kate's. She had always been a reserved, shy young woman; yet now she threw caution to the winds, thrust her way through the crowd and hugged me tight. In all my nineteen and a half years she was the first young woman to give me a kiss—I didn't count Gran and Mrs Maisky. It made me blush—and her too.

'We did it!' she said, flushed with pride and pleasure.

She was right to take some of the glory. If it hadn't been for her patience and unselfish help I wouldn't have got into the music school in the first place. But Kate had a rival for my body. I heard the swish of her wings before I was swept up in a flurry of feathers. This time I need not have feared for my poor clarinet because Mrs Maisky had a surprise for me.

'Beelee, you deserve present.'

She handed me a long, oblong gift-wrapped box. But before I could open it, she had snatched it back, tearing off the paper to reveal a black clarinet case; then opening the case she exclaimed, 'Ees for you.'

Even as I began to thank her, she had turned her attentions to Hai Ren who disappeared under her vast wings, like a brood of chicks under the mother hen. I hoped she had not brought him a grand piano as a present—I could imagine her carrying it in and dropping it on him!

125

Her place in the crowd was taken by the pink round face of Alexander Maisky who just beamed and beamed, gold teeth flashing in the chandelier light.

'Villiam, I vont you to meet somevon,' he said.

He ushered forward a thin, distinguished-looking man who held out a hand and spoke in a strong foreign accent.

'Congratulations, young man. I like your playing. Please take my card: I wish to speak with you.'

Was this the first lead to a musical career? It certainly sent my pulses racing. But Mr Maisky's next words immediately turned joy to bitter disappointment.

'Mr Goldblum is Principal Conductor with the Hamburg Symphony Orchestra; he has come specially from Germany to hear you.'

A German! For years I had stored up hatred of the very name. German meant my mother's murder, the cause of my agony and scars. How could I play in Germany, with Germans?

Mr Goldblum noticed the shadow of pain cross my face. He obviously knew my background.

'William, I know what the name German means to you. To me it means far more: I was born there and I love my country and my fellow Germans. I love Beethoven and Brahms. But I also hate those Germans who caused the war, the death and suffering of six million of my fellow Jews, including all my family. However, musicians like you and me, we have no boundaries, we are a world family, we can teach others peace and toleration.'

I kept silent. This needed more thought. But I promised to meet him next day.

The Maiskys and their friend moved on to mingle with fellow guests, while I took the chance to grab a drink and sausage roll. As I turned my back on the room, I heard a familiar voice behind me, 'Hey up, lad. Tha did greet.'

This was the man who had given me hope, the will to live and earn respect; I loved this man more than any other. And I owed him everything.

'Terry,' I said warmly. 'You came . . . '

As I turned, I was surprised and embarrassed to see someone by his side, the prettiest woman I'd ever seen. It had to be Mary. It couldn't be anyone else.

'Hello, Billy,' she said. 'I've heard so much about you.'

'Thanks for coming,' I said. 'You've made my day.'

I could hardly contain myself: the emotions of love and music are so close; to combine the two was almost too much.

We pushed our way through the crowd to some chairs in the corner, and we chatted for some fifteen minutes before they had to leave.

I received my second young lady's kiss of the evening and returned Terry's firm handshake without a grimace.

'Ouch!' he said in mock agony. 'I told thee playing music'd make thee strong.'

'Strong in mind as well as body,' I replied.

'Then tell others,' he said warmly. 'Write a book about it. Give hope to t'less fortunate.'

I made no promises. I was better at music than at words.

With that we parted. To think that once I had doubted his very existence!

Left alone I searched the room for other familiar faces. I knew that Iris and Fred were tied up with their children, though they'd sent me a long letter and invited me to stay with them after graduation. I was sad and disappointed not to see Hilary or anyone from the Home—but I understood how hard it is to venture into the outside world. In the years to come I would return to the Home several times to talk and play my clarinet.

The next few days were spent in a busy whirl of

packing, visiting, and thinking over my future. I had two offers to join an orchestra—the second was for closer home, not far from Iris and Fred. After giving it much thought, I finally plumped for Germany. I liked challenges, and this promised to be one of the greatest challenges of my life.

My only contact with Germans so far was the war; and the only German I'd ever met was Mr Goldblum. I'd read somewhere that not all the German people supported Hitler; even those who believed in a master race might now be having second thoughts—like the English with faith in Empire and the white man's right to rule.

I'd had a bellyful of prejudice myself, yet here I was having to cope with my own, against Germans. I knew it wasn't right to hate them all. Maybe through music I could build bridges, create more than musical harmony. For that I needed to understand why people feel the way they do. There must be lots of ordinary Germans who wanted to be friends: after all, if you're really friendly with someone, you don't want to go around killing them, do you?

That sounds a bit pompous. Yet like many teenagers after the war, I was looking for a mission: to mend fences, to set aside the prejudices of our parents, to learn and understand. I recalled something I'd read in a Russian book which Mr Maisky once gave me— Tolstoy's *War and Peace*: 'If evil people can come together and make war, why can't good people, who are infinitely more numerous, get together to bring peace?'

It sounded so simple. And it *was* simple. My choice had to be Germany.

Among the many letters of congratulation that arrived, two were especially precious. The first was from dear old Whiteway, the plastic surgeon who had worked so long to give me a face.

Dear William,

Thank you for the kind invitation to your concert. I enjoyed it hugely. I was especially pleased to see you breathing cleanly through your nose. Judging by your pianist friend, you have reaped the benefit of Oriental medicine. Wise people, the Chinese. Always put health first.

I'm not a terribly sociable man, so I didn't stop to mix and mingle. I can say what I need to say better on paper. A few years ago I told you I wasn't a mender of men's souls. I'm not. If one hasn't the will-power, no end of operations will put one right. But you found the will and have mended yourself.

It is success like yours that makes my life's work worthwhile. Thank you, my boy.

Yours,

Arthur Whiteway

How odd. In all those years I never knew dear old 'Whitewash' had a first name: Arthur. With a wry smile I recalled his advice to abandon my clarinet. So doctors aren't always right! Perhaps that's what he meant by 'mending yourself'. It was very kind of him to come to the concert and to write, and so typical not to stay.

The second letter came with an Edinburgh postmark; the envelope was pink and smelt of carnations. I knew the writer at once from the address: 'William J. Riley, Esq.' She always wrote that. Her letter was long and moving.

Dear Billy,

Or should I call you 'William' now that you're famous? I didn't need to come to your concert to know you'd win something; I've always had faith in you, even before you had faith in yourself. In any case, I had my own first-year university exams—which, you'll be surprised to learn, I not only passed, I came top in.

We didn't get off to a good start, you and I, did we? Let's be honest: you detested me, and I'm not really surprised. I was a right little madam, thinking I had the answer to everyone's problems, driving you nuts with my wireless and gramophone.

But I desperately wanted to get through to you. Do you remember those fairy cakes I used to bake? Sometimes I felt like putting poison in them, you were so rude, so full of self pity and uncaring about the rest of us. Yet I knew you enjoyed my little presents. Then there was THAT BOOK. Sometimes I'm a bit envious that you and not I met Terry Clough. But it's all turned out fine, hasn't it?

When you started playing the clarinet I was half pleased and half driven mad by the racket. But the music changed you, gave you confidence and patience. I began to love the new person who emerged from the cocoon, and I felt proud that I had made a tiny contribution. Most of all, I loved the way you started to care for others. Do you recall the time you spent the first money you earned on flowers for me? That moved me to tears.

I wish you were still my neighbour, but you wouldn't fancy an ugly mug like me. In any case, our lives have moved apart. I shall be a surgeon one day, maybe helping to mould new faces, giving something back to those who helped us. And you—when you're famous I'll be able to tell my children that the world-renowned clarinettist William J. Riley was once my neighbour. I'll be so proud and I'll love you all the more.

Much love,
Hilary

I folded the letter and put it into my inside pocket, next to my heart. I badly needed fresh air, solitude, a walk in the woods.

CONGRATULATIONS

For hours I wandered with nothing but the breeze, birds, and butterflies for company. I was deep in thought, going over the events of my life: the bomb, the operations, the Home, the music school, the concert—and all the people I'd met along the way.

Before returning to the house, I paused for a moment and looked around: at the sky, the leafy trees, the summer flowers, the ladybirds and butterflies. Fondly I patted Hilary's letter.

'Billy boy, life isn't so bad after all.'

Other Oxford Fiction

Witchy
Ann Phillips
ISBN 0 19 275049 6

They said she was a witch, and threw her out of the village. Wherever Aggie goes and whatever she does, she can't escape the gossip that follows her.

She finds a new home and begins a new life. But just when Aggie thinks her troubles are behind her, the past comes back to haunt her—and she's thrust back into a life of superstition and hate . . .

'This latest offering from Ann Phillips, will cast a spell from beginning to end.'
The Times

'. . . the novel grows to a chilling climax and satisfying conclusion.'
The Daily Telegraph

The School That Went On Strike
Pamela Scobie
ISBN 0 19 275051 8

'What can you do? Nobody listens to children.'
'Oh, no? Then we'll MAKE them listen! If the grown-ups won't go on strike—WE WILL!'

And that's exactly what Violet and the rest of the pupils at Burston School do. They are fed up with the way their teachers have been treated and decide that there is only one way to make themselves heard . . .

Based on true events, this is the story of a group of children who come together to fight for goodness and justice—it's the story of the school that went on strike.

The Throttlepenny Murder
Roger Green
ISBN 0 19 275052 6

Jessie hated old Throttlepenny, her mean-spirited boss. She spent her days dreaming of ways to hurt him, but she'd never have the nerve to turn her dreams into reality.

But Throttlepenny is murdered. It's Jessie that the police come for, and Jessie that winds up in jail. Will someone prove her innocence—before she's hanged?

Flambards
K. M. Peyton
ISBN 0 19 275024 0

Twelve-year-old Christina is sent to live in a decaying old mansion with her fierce uncle and his two sons. She soon discovers a passion for horses and riding, but she has to become part of a strange family. This brooding household is divided by emotional undercurrents and cruelty . . .

Chartbreak
Gillian Cross
ISBN 0 19 275043 7

When Janis Finch storms out of a family row, it starts a chain of events which transforms her whole life. For it's in the motorway café, minutes later, that she meets the unknown rock band, Kelp, who talk her into coming to their gig that night.

Janis goes along for the ride, and finds herself increasingly provoked by Christie, Kelp's arrogant lead singer. He pushes her into singing with them, and winds her up into a fever of rage, awe, and attraction. So when Christie asks her to join the band, Janis feels powerless to refuse—and her life explodes.

Against the Day
Michael Cronin
ISBN 0 19 275039 9

It is 1940. The Nazis have invaded, and Britain is now part of the Third Reich. All over the country, German military authorities are taking control, led by the brutal Gestapo.

But slowly, surely, a resistance is building throughout the land. A secret network of people are plotting to overthrow the Nazis and win back their freedom, at any cost. Frank and Les, two schoolboys, never meant to get involved—but find themselves part of a dangerous undercover operation that can only end in bloodshed . . .

Chandra
Frances Mary Hendry
ISBN 0 19 275058 5
Winner of the Writer's Guild Award and the Lancashire Book Award

Chandra can't believe her luck. The boy her parents have chosen for her to marry seems to be modern and open-minded. She's sure they will have a wonderful life together. So once they are married she travels out to the desert to live with him and his family—only when she gets there, things are not as she imagined.

Alone in her darkened room she tries to keep her strength and her identity. She is Chandra and she won't let it be forgotten.

River Boy
Tim Bowler
ISBN 0 19 275035 6
Winner of the Carnegie Medal

Standing at the top of the fall, framed against the sky, was the figure of a boy. At least, it looked like a boy, though he was quite tall and it was hard to make out his features against the glare of the sun. She watched and waited, uncertain what to do, and whether she had been seen.

When Jess's grandfather has a serious heart attack, surely their planned trip to his boyhood home will have to be cancelled? But Grandpa insists on going so that he can finish his final painting, 'River Boy'. As Jess helps her ailing grandfather with his work, she becomes entranced by the scene he is painting. And then she becomes aware of a strange presence in the river, the figure of a boy, asking her for help and issuing a challenge that will stretch her swimming talents to the limits. But can she take up the challenge before it is too late for Grandpa . . . and the River Boy?

It's My Life
Michael Harrison
ISBN 0 19 275042 9

As soon as he opens his front door, Martin feels that something's wrong. But he never expects the hand over his mouth, the rope around his wrists, and the mysterious man who's after a large ransom. Before Martin knows it, he's a pawn in a dangerous game that becomes more and more terrifying with every turn . . .